Copyright © 2024 by Steve Hutchison
All rights reserved. No part of this publication may be reproduced, distributed, or transmitted in any form or by any means, including photocopying, recording, or other electronic or mechanical methods, without the prior written permission of the publisher, except in the case of brief quotations used for purposes of review, commentary, or scholarly analysis.

First Edition, 2024
ISBN-13: 978-1778872792

Published by Tales of Terror
Website: https://terror.ca
Social Media: @terrorca

Steve Hutchison – steve@shade.ca
Bookstores and wholesalers: Please contact books@terror.ca

PREFACE

Welcome to Creepypasta Land. Within these pages lie 20 of my most chilling stories, carefully crafted to plunge you into the depths of fear and imagination. What began as viral prompts designed to spread unease has evolved into fully fleshed-out tales that will grip you from start to finish.

Each story is paired with haunting illustrations that draw you deeper into a world where the familiar twists into the uncanny. From creeping psychological dread to spine-chilling supernatural encounters, these tales will stay with you long after the final page, making you question the boundaries of reality and imagination.

Prepare yourself for a journey into darkness where nothing is as it seems. I hope these stories linger in your mind, just as they haunted mine. Enter at your own risk—and enjoy the ride.

Steve Hutchison

STORIES

7. Chef Fleshmore

13. 3AM Boy

19. Naked Garden

25. Uncontrollable Laughter

31. Sticky Notes

37. Twofold Harbinger

43. Last Valentine

49. Sunflower Grin

55. Canyon Crypt

61. Bad Product

67. Strange Student

73. Tree Hunter

79. Graveyard Triad

85. Mister Midnight

91. Nowhere Stairs

97. Emoji Max

103. Brainstorm Lullaby

109. Grim Exit

115. Screaming Lily

121. Static Black

Chef Fleshmore

The story of Chef Fleshmore had traveled through whispers for years. In a shadowed corner of downtown, hidden between flickering neon and crumbling alleys, stood a teppanyaki restaurant like no other. Its name was forgotten by most, but the chef—everyone remembered him.

Chef Fleshmore was a legend. His bright white coat, splashed with garish reds and yellows made him impossible to miss. He dazzled with his knife tricks, but it was his smile—the kind that didn't reach his eyes—that stayed with customers. They said his "special beef" was the best they'd ever tasted—tender, savory, unlike anything they'd had. Some swore it tasted... wrong, but no one dared ask. They just came back.

For newlyweds Jamie and Lisa, the allure was irresistible. On their honeymoon, a friend swore the food was life-changing. Eager for something extraordinary, they entered the dimly lit space, greeted by the chef himself.

"Welcome! You're in for a treat!" Fleshmore grinned, leading them to their seats near the grill, the sizzling sounds filling the air.

As he worked, Jamie and Lisa drank more than they should. The grill sizzled, the meat browned just right, but something felt off. The texture was too smooth. The color... too perfect. Jamie shook it off, blaming the wine.

Lisa stopped mid-chew. "What... is this?" she whispered, staring at her plate.

Jamie glanced at the meat. Too soft. Almost... alive.

Fleshmore's grin never wavered. "The finest beef you'll ever taste," he said. "One of a kind."

They exchanged uneasy glances, but their hunger overcame their doubts. "More," Jamie slurred, waving his hand.

"Of course," Fleshmore replied, his smile deepening. He disappeared into the back.

The couple sat in tense silence. Fleshmore returned moments later, his smile even wider. He moved to the grill, his hands steady—too steady. With exaggerated flourish, he began cooking the meat. The sizzle filled the room, but his performance was unnerving. He tossed vegetables into the air, flames flaring up. His movements were smooth, almost too perfect. The meat browned just right—too perfectly—as he plated it, his smile never fading.

Jamie cleared his throat. "Where's it come from?"

Fleshmore looked at the kitchen door. "Special beef. The best you'll ever have."

Fleshmore stepped back into the kitchen. The fridge door creaked open. A low hum filled the air, unnatural. Jamie couldn't see beyond it, but the silence felt too long. A brief flash of metal caught his eye before the door slammed shut. Fleshmore returned with freshly cut meat from the fridge. "The best," he murmured, his voice dark.

The mass. The thing in the fridge. It was alive, stretching beyond its limits. Fleshmore had to cut it back, keep it in check, or it might consume the entire space. But it was becoming more of a convenience. No need to buy or order meat anymore. His customers—curious, eager to taste the legendary beef—kept coming back, lured by the mystery of it all. And so, the restaurant stayed open, its business thriving on a never-ending supply.

Jamie and Lisa ate, oblivious. Fleshmore lingered in the kitchen's shadows, eyes fixed on them, watching every bite. He didn't need more customers. He only needed the mass kept in check. Or else...

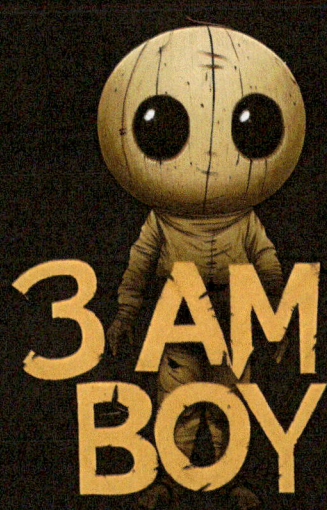

3 AM BOY

Every night, at exactly 3 AM, Fanny woke up with a start, her heart pounding. It always began the same way: a faint creaking noise in the house, just loud enough to pull her from sleep. It never woke her parents or little brother, who slept down the hall. It was like the house knew only Fanny could hear it. After a week of sleepless nights, curiosity took over.

Tonight, she decided to investigate.

Fanny crept out of bed and tiptoed down the hallway. The bathroom and kitchen were quiet, everything in place. But when she reached the living room, her breath caught in her throat.

There, sitting on the couch, was a small figure. No taller than two feet, it looked like a little boy, but something was wrong. His body was made of smooth, dark wood, like a doll. His clothes were torn and brown. And his eyes—black,

shiny orbs that never blinked, always staring. For a moment, Fanny couldn't move. The wooden boy sat still, waiting for her. Then, he turned his head toward her with a sudden jerk.

"Are you the 3 AM Boy?" she whispered, her voice trembling.

The boy tilted his head and repeated softly, "3 AM Boy."

Fanny stepped back, but something about him felt oddly... innocent. He wasn't threatening. He just was.

"Follow me," the boy said, holding out his small hand.

Without thinking, Fanny followed him down the hallway, up the stairs, and into the attic. He crawled into a narrow opening in the wall—an old tunnel she remembered using as a child to access the condemned section of the attic. Back then, it had been a secret passage, hidden away in the forgotten parts of the house. She hesitated. She was too big now, but the boy's voice called her forward.

"Come," he urged. "I have treasures to show you."

Something in his voice made Fanny crawl into the tunnel. She emerged into a forgotten corner of the attic, and what she saw made her freeze.

Piled around her were all the things she had lost over the years—old toys, broken dolls, clothes she'd outgrown. It was like a graveyard of her childhood, a place where time had stopped.

She stood there for a moment, running her fingers over the forgotten treasures. A strange feeling washed over her—a pull, something that made her want to stay. She could feel the boy's presence behind her, his eyes following her every movement. Fanny turned toward the tunnel, ready to leave. But when she reached for it, the opening was gone. The attic was silent, the space around her cold and empty. The boy was still there, standing perfectly still, his black eyes locked on hers.

"What should we play?" he asked, his voice soft, like the creak of old wood.

Fanny's breath caught in her throat. There was no escape. The tunnel, the way out—everything had disappeared. The boy wasn't just strange—he was part of the house, part of something she couldn't understand.

And in that moment, Fanny realized with chilling clarity:

She wasn't leaving. Not ever.

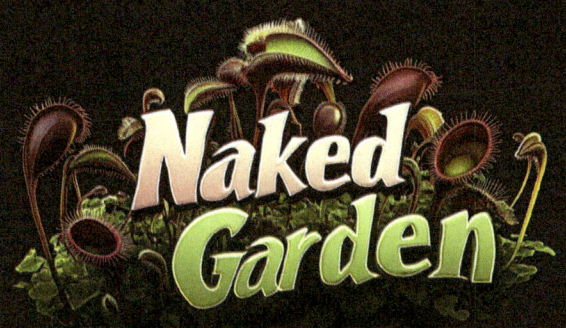

Naked Garden

Brian was desperate to join the fraternity at his fancy college—the one his parents spent a fortune on. It wasn't about brotherhood or school spirit. No, this frat was his golden ticket to the football team, and Brian wasn't going to let it slip by. So, when the brothers told him about the initiation challenge, he pushed down his nerves and agreed.

They led him to an old, rundown house just off campus, rumored to belong to a "crazy plant lady". Her front yard was a tangled mess of wild greenery, with thick vines, sharp brambles, strange flowers, and giant, swollen pods. Everywhere he looked, Brian saw odd plants with thick, fleshy stems and open mouths—plants that looked a little too much like they were watching him. The brothers called them "carnivorous" and laughed like it was some big joke.

The rules were simple, they said, grinning. Brian had to strip down—completely—and find the football they'd hidden somewhere in that jungle of weird plants. Oh, and he had to

do it without getting "eaten," they joked, elbowing each other. Brian chuckled along, even though his heart was pounding. This was just a dumb prank, right? Nothing dangerous. Nothing real.

So he did it. He stripped, shivering even in the warm noon sun, feeling more exposed than ever before. The leader of the frat tossed the football. It bounced off the house's crooked porch and vanished somewhere in the thick undergrowth. Brian hesitated, then stepped forward, trying to ignore the strange plants that seemed to lean towards him as he moved. He wanted this over with as quickly as possible, so he dropped to a crouch, crawling through the weeds, wincing as thorns scraped against his bare skin.

Minutes dragged on. He was muttering under his breath, feeling more and more frustrated, when his fingers suddenly touched something smooth and solid—the football! Relief washed over him. But when he stood up, he froze.

A shadow loomed over him. It was a plant, not like the others—a huge, towering thing that seemed to have come out of nowhere. Its enormous mouth, ringed with jagged, blood-red petals, hung open right in front of him. It had looked like just another bush before, blending into the wild mess of the garden, but now it was alive, standing tall and blocking out the sun. The brothers' laughter stopped all at once. Brian's breath caught. He took a step back, clutching the ball, but the ground beneath him shifted.

The plant moved. It lunged.

The last thing Brian saw was that terrible, gaping mouth as it snapped shut, and the last thing he heard was the strangled, terrified gasps of the brothers. They didn't stick around to help. They bolted back to campus, not daring to look back.

The next day, they said it had all been a dumb prank—a joke that had gotten out of hand. They whispered about it sometimes, late at night, but no one ever spoke Brian's name out loud during the day. There was no record of him joining the frat. No one ever saw him leave the house.

The story of Brian turned into a tradition—a scary tale to spook new pledges each year. But every now and then, when the wind rustled through the overgrown yard, some claimed they could hear a faint voice, almost like a whisper, carried through the thick leaves:

"I just wanted to play."

Uncontrollable Laughter

Avery was late. Her job interview downtown was only minutes away, and the taxi she'd called was crawling through a river of stalled cars. She tapped her fingers anxiously on the window, her eyes darting between the clock on her phone and the endless line of vehicles. That's when she noticed it—a faint swirl of pink in the sky.

It wasn't like a normal fog. The smoke seemed... alive. It twisted in spirals, thick and syrupy, curling down from the heavens like the fingers of some unseen hand. Before Avery could say a word, the pink haze seeped through the taxi's vents.

Her laughter started small, almost like a hiccup. "Hah... ha..." Then it grew louder. And louder.

Her ribs ached as she threw her head back, cackling uncontrollably. Tears streamed down her face, but they weren't from joy. There was nothing funny—nothing at all.

The laughter was wrong, an alien force that clawed at her throat. She could feel her body betraying her, convulsing with every sinister guffaw.

The driver wasn't faring any better; he was doubled over the steering wheel, choking on his own maniacal giggles.

Avery's lungs burned. She scrambled for the door handle and stumbled onto the street, gasping for air. But outside was no sanctuary. The pink mist coated everything, thick and oppressive. All around her, people were collapsing—hands clutching at their sides, faces twisted in unnatural grins. Some had stopped moving altogether, their smiles frozen in eerie stillness.

She ran. Her legs pumped wildly, her laughter breaking into wheezing sobs as her breath failed her. Every street was the same: people collapsing, twitching, or clawing at their throats, their eyes bulging in panicked terror. No one could stop laughing.

The hospital came into view—a towering structure of glass and steel, a beacon of hope. She sprinted toward it, weaving between fallen bodies and gasping for relief. Surely, surely someone there could help.

But the moment she burst through the sliding doors, that hope was crushed. Nurses were doubled over, their masks slipping as they howled in helpless mirth. Patients in wheelchairs convulsed with uncontrollable giggles. Even the doctors—those pillars of reason—were on their knees, clutching

their stomachs as peals of laughter echoed through the sterile halls.

The sound was unbearable, a symphony of despair disguised as joy. It filled her ears, reverberating in her skull like a sickening chorus. The mist had won.

Through the haze, Avery caught her reflection in a fractured glass door. Her face was unfamiliar—eyes wide with panic, lips pulled into a grin too wide, too strained. She looked like a doll, a mockery of herself.

And still, the laughter came.

Somewhere in the depths of her mind, one thought clawed its way to the surface: this wasn't just an accident. The pink smoke wasn't random. It was a curse. A plague of laughter meant to torment, to consume.

As her vision blurred and her chest heaved, Avery felt herself falling to the ground. Her body shook with the force of the laughter, her last breath slipping away in a soundless scream disguised as a giggle.

The city was silent now, save for the lingering echoes of a joke no one would ever understand.

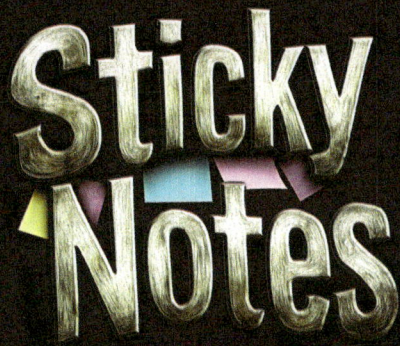

Sticky Notes

Bridget had always been organized. As a data scientist working from home, she liked things tidy. Every file named, every task scheduled. But when her doctor told her she had a degenerative disease that would steal her memory, she turned to sticky notes.

She started with a notepad, but it was slow to flip through. Sticky notes were better—bright and quick to read. Soon, they covered her office walls, each note a reminder of something important.

At first, she used a simple color system: blue for work, yellow for errands, pink for health. But soon, she forgot what the colors meant.

Frustrated, she taped a master list in the hallway, explaining her color code. That was supposed to fix everything, but it only made things worse. The hallway became an extension of her memory, a guide to her own mind. More sticky

notes appeared—then more. They migrated from the office to the kitchen, bathroom, bedroom. Every inch of space became covered. The notes were her lifeline, the only way to hold onto slipping fragments of her life.

She stopped leaving the house. It was easier that way. She forgot how to get to the grocery store, so she ordered delivery. Her shopping list was pinned to the front door—on a sticky note, of course. Her computer files grew chaotic; she couldn't keep them straight anymore. The sticky notes became a crutch, a way to manage her disintegrating mind.

One night, she woke in darkness, disoriented. Her window was blocked by a wall of sticky notes, and the room felt alien, almost hostile. Heart pounding, she stumbled into the hallway. Her bare feet slipped on fallen notes, their edges sharp and cold. She grabbed the walls, trying to steady herself.

She tore a note from the wall: "Don't forget—" it read, but the ink was smudged and faded. Another said, "Remember this!" but there was nothing to remember, nothing but a hollow echo of urgency.

The hallway seemed to close in on her, suffocating. The notes climbed higher, layer upon layer, merging into a dizzying blur of colors. The walls themselves seemed to breathe, the paper rustling with the slightest touch. She felt a tightness in her chest, like the weight of the notes was pressing down on her.

She shuffled forward, her feet crunching on the paper underfoot. Her fingers brushed over dozens of notes, desperate to find something that made sense.

She couldn't. They were only fragments—lists, warnings, names she didn't recognize anymore. Her mind felt as cluttered as the house, her thoughts as fragmented as the walls of paper.

She moved through the living room, wading through drifts of sticky notes. They stuck to her hands, her clothes, her hair. Each note was meaningless, yet they clung to her like they had a purpose she'd forgotten.

The house was a maze, a trap of her own making. The notes had taken over, whispering nonsense, filling the silence with a soft, maddening rustle. She knew she should be scared, but all she felt was a strange, hollow comfort in their presence. They were beautiful, in a way—like stars against the darkness, each one catching the dim light.

But none of them could tell her what she'd lost. They only held the traces of a life that no longer belonged to her.

Twofold Harbinger

A year had passed since the carnival, but Olivia couldn't forget that night. She and Emma had snuck in, not for rides or games, but for the fortune-telling tent. Their mother's diagnosis had left them desperate, and rumors about the tent's strange predictions were too tempting to ignore. It wasn't really a tent—just a worn wooden shack painted with faded stripes. Olivia led the way inside, her heart pounding.

The air was heavy with incense, and at the center of the room stood the fortune-teller. It had two heads. The left one grinned broadly, alive with expression. The right was still and solemn, its gaze fixed.

"Come in," the left head said, its voice sing-song. "You're here to see."

"To learn," added the right, low and calm.

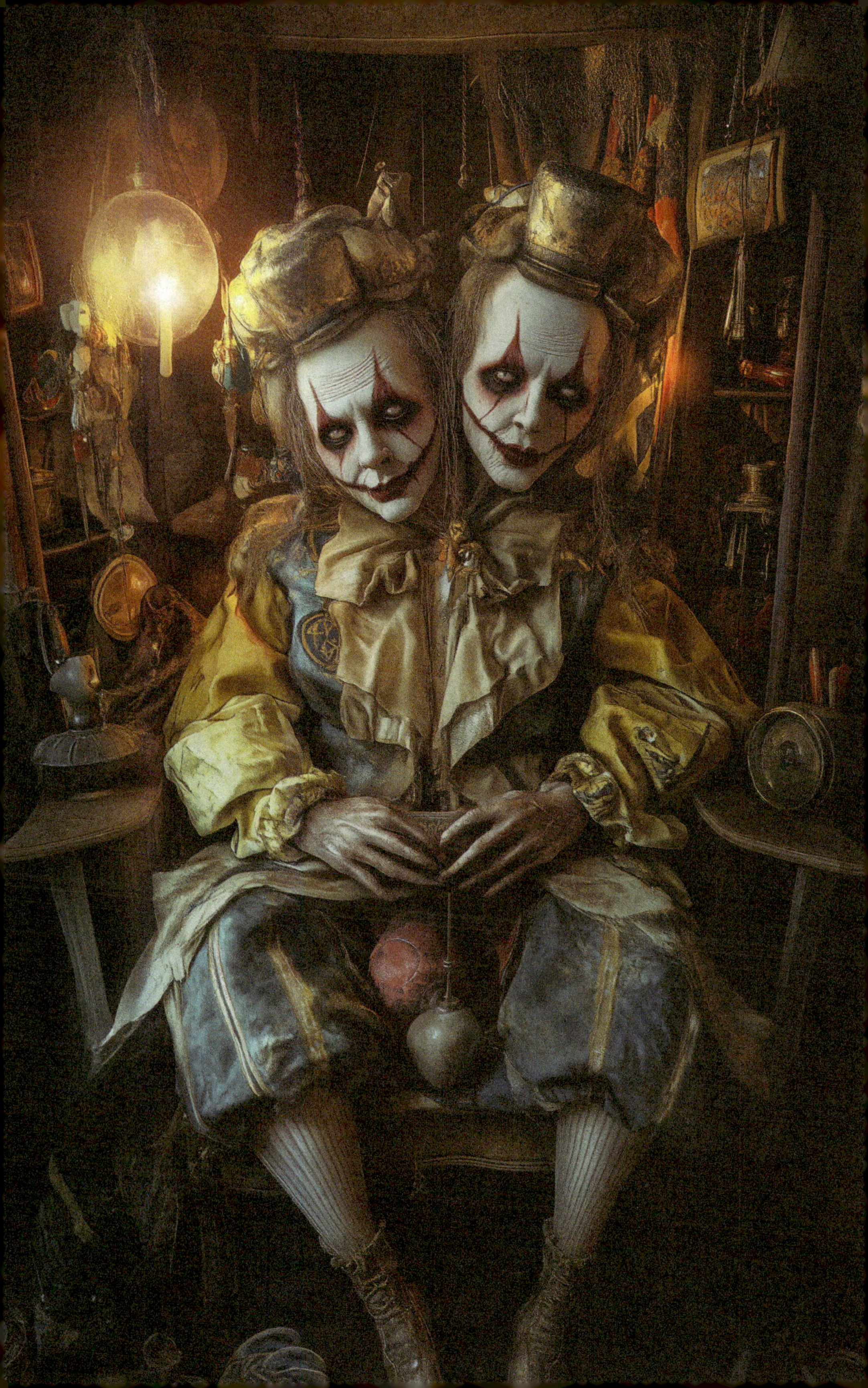

Olivia swallowed hard. "It's about our mom. She's sick. We want to know what'll happen."

"For a dollar," said the left, leaning closer. "Two futures. One is true."

"And one is false," the right finished. "Decide for yourself."

Hesitant, Olivia handed over her dollar. The jester snapped its fingers, conjuring two glowing orbs—one red, one blue. The orbs spun, glowing brighter, then stilled. The red orb shimmered, showing their mother surrounded by sunlight and flowers in a vibrant field. The blue darkened, revealing storm clouds and an empty hospital bed. Olivia's breath caught as the images disappeared.

"Two paths," the left head said cheerfully.

"Which one is real?" Olivia asked, desperate.

"Time reveals the truth," said the right. "The truth leaves its mark."

Before she could press further, the orbs reappeared, sharper this time. In the red orb, their mother lay pale and still in a hospital bed. In the blue orb, she was older, her silver-streaked hair catching the light as she smiled warmly. The images vanished just as quickly.

"Tell me how to make the good one happen!" Olivia begged.

"Another dollar," said the left head.

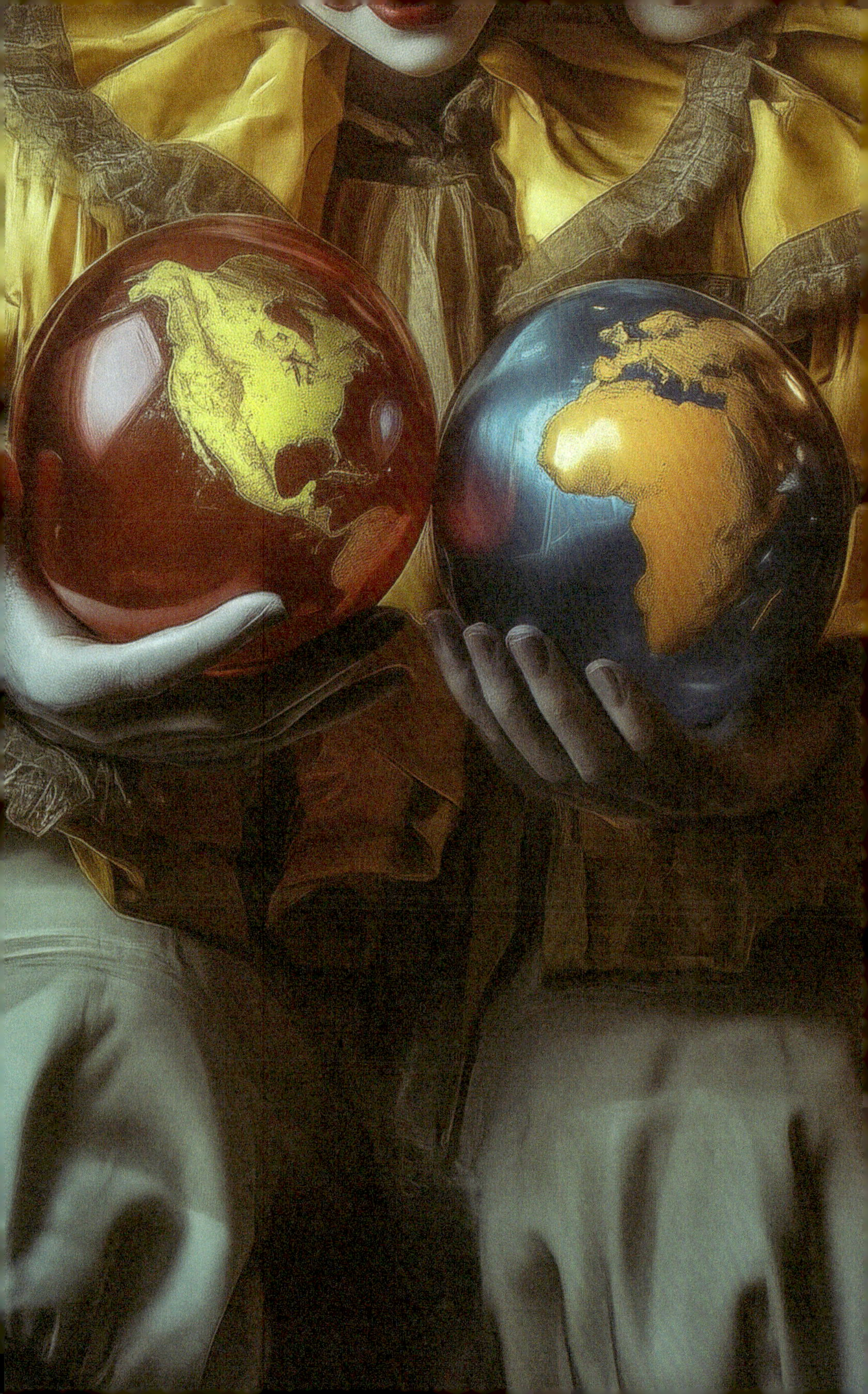

"I don't have one!" Olivia's voice broke as she frantically searched her pockets.

The jester's faces softened slightly. "No dollar, no divination," said the right. "The price isn't ours to change."

"This isn't about me! It's about her!" Olivia shouted.

The two heads exchanged a glance. "The truth is yours to find," the right said quietly. "We'll meet again in four years."

The tent dimmed, and Olivia found herself outside. Emma clung to her arm, and they walked home in silence. In the weeks that followed, Olivia searched obsessively for signs. She analyzed every cough, every smile, and saw patterns everywhere: a hospital brochure on a sidewalk, a stranger's scarf that reminded her of her mom's. Were these the marks of truth, or just coincidences?

Even now, a year later, Olivia watched and waited, hoping she could find the answer—and that she still had time to change it.

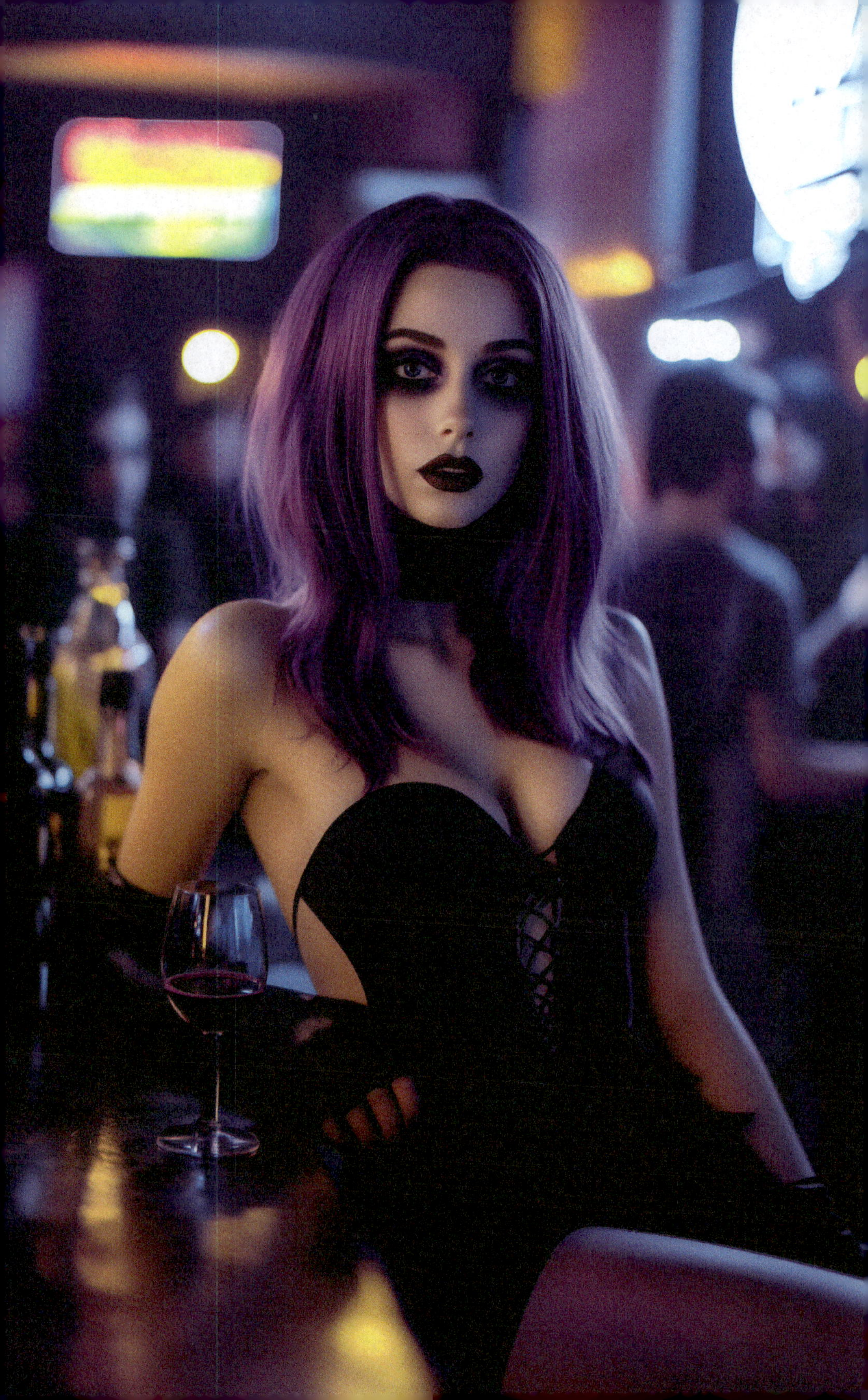

Last Valentine

On Valentine's Day, Sean met Gemma at Tidal, a prestigious New York City nightclub adorned with a purple octopus logo.

He had been invited by a close friend—a woman he'd wronged in the past but who had seemingly forgiven him. Or had she? Sometimes he caught a flicker of something in her eyes: resentment, perhaps, or maybe his own guilt playing tricks.

She wasn't there when he arrived, so he waited at the bar. That's when Gemma walked in. Stunning, enigmatic, with long purple hair and a sleek black dress, she exuded effortless allure.

She slid onto the stool beside him, feigning indifference, but Sean recognized the subtle cues of interest—her side-eye, her posture.

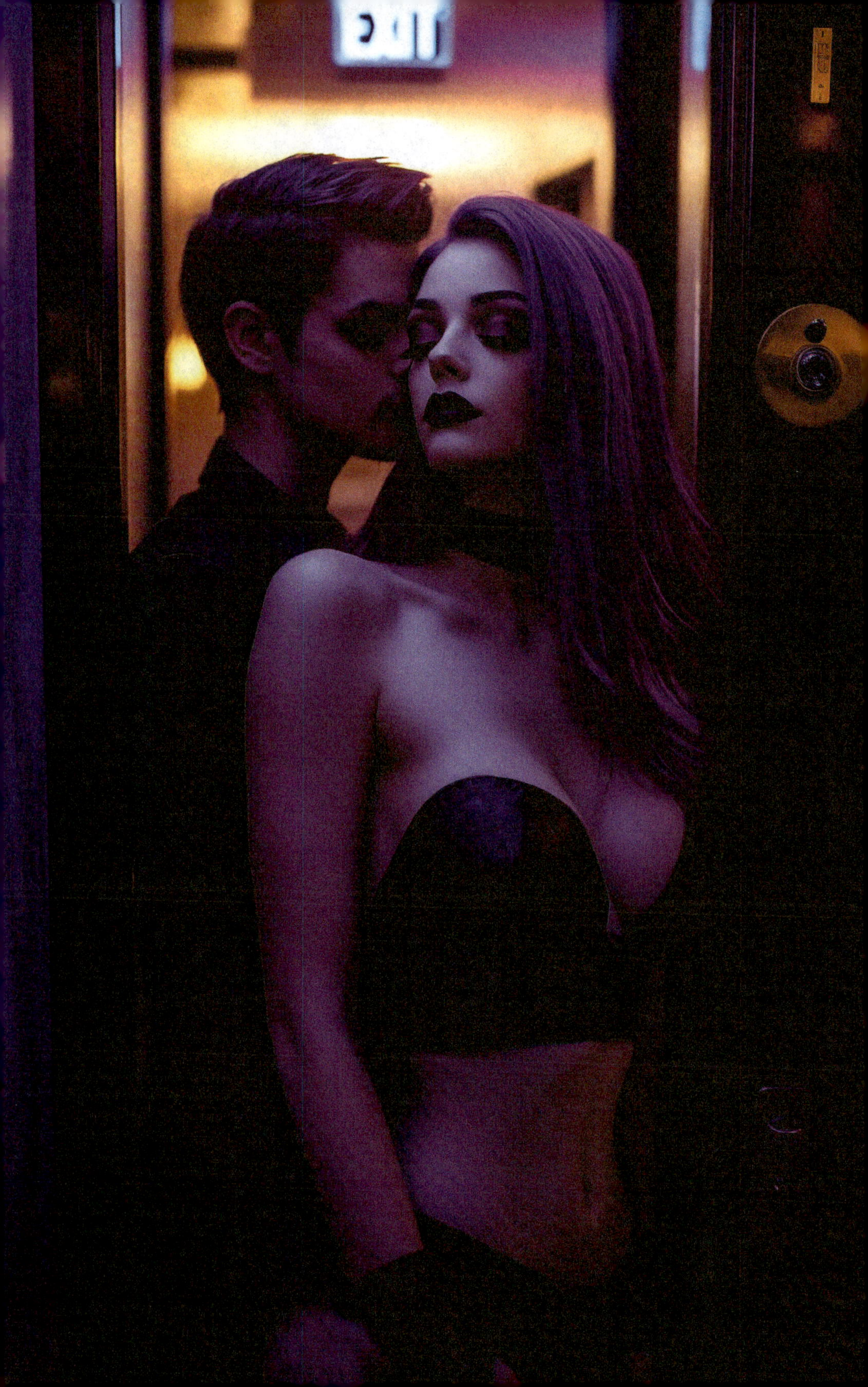

A seasoned charmer, Sean broke the ice with a casual, friendly remark. To his surprise, Gemma was more open than anyone he'd ever met—warm, but not flirtatious, and oddly disarming.

They shared a bottle of wine, then another. Sean was drawn to her in ways he couldn't quite explain. When the bartender handed them two peculiar condom-like pouches, he hesitated. "Orgasm?" the bartender murmured, sliding the packets across the counter. Sean recognized the name—a rare and whispered-about street drug—but Gemma didn't blink.

She tore hers open, revealing a small pill stamped with the same octopus logo as the nightclub's door. Caught up in her confidence, Sean followed suit.

Time blurred. An hour later, they wandered down an ornate hallway that opened into a vast, vacant lobby with towering windows and dim lighting. It was eerily silent, as though the club's energy had vanished behind them.

They kissed, the intensity of the moment heightened by the mysterious drug coursing through their veins. Sean suggested going to Gemma's apartment, and she agreed, but just as they turned to leave, something... shifted.

Gemma doubled over, clutching her stomach. "Something's wrong," she gasped. Her body convulsed, her breathing ragged.

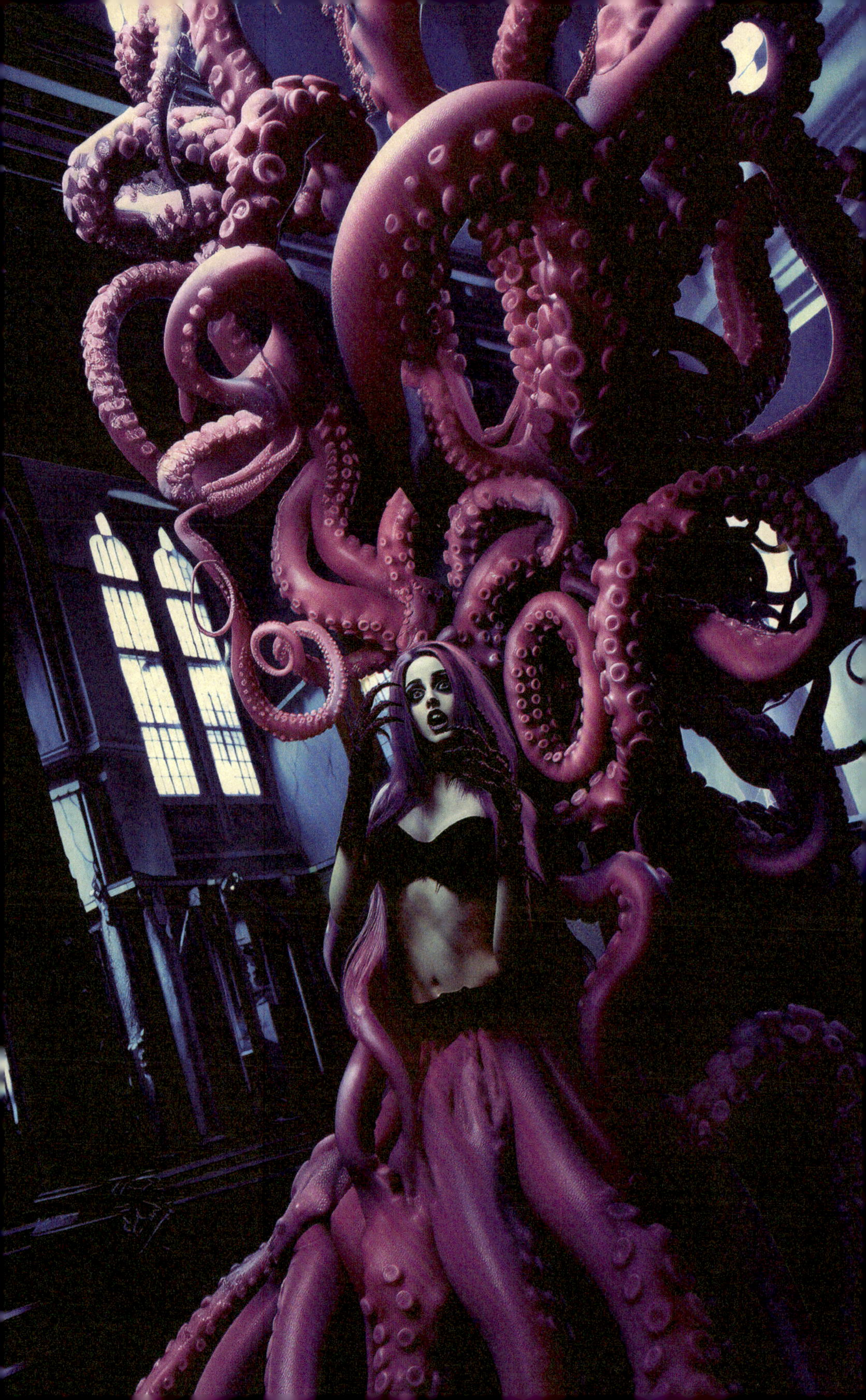

Sean watched in frozen horror as slimy appendages sprouted from her back, writhing and growing with impossible speed. Her terrified eyes locked onto his. "What's happening to me?" she choked out, her voice a mix of agony and despair. Her once-beautiful face began to twist, her features softening and elongating unnaturally.

Sean stumbled backward, his heart pounding. A terrible realization struck him like a cold wave: the drug. It wasn't just a high—it was a transformation.

He glanced down at his own trembling hands, his veins darkening beneath his skin. It was only a matter of time before it happened to him, too.

Gemma's screams echoed in the empty lobby, her new tentacles lashing against the polished marble floor.

Sean felt the first twinge deep inside him—a sharp, alien pull—reminding him that he wasn't just a witness to this nightmare. He was its next victim.

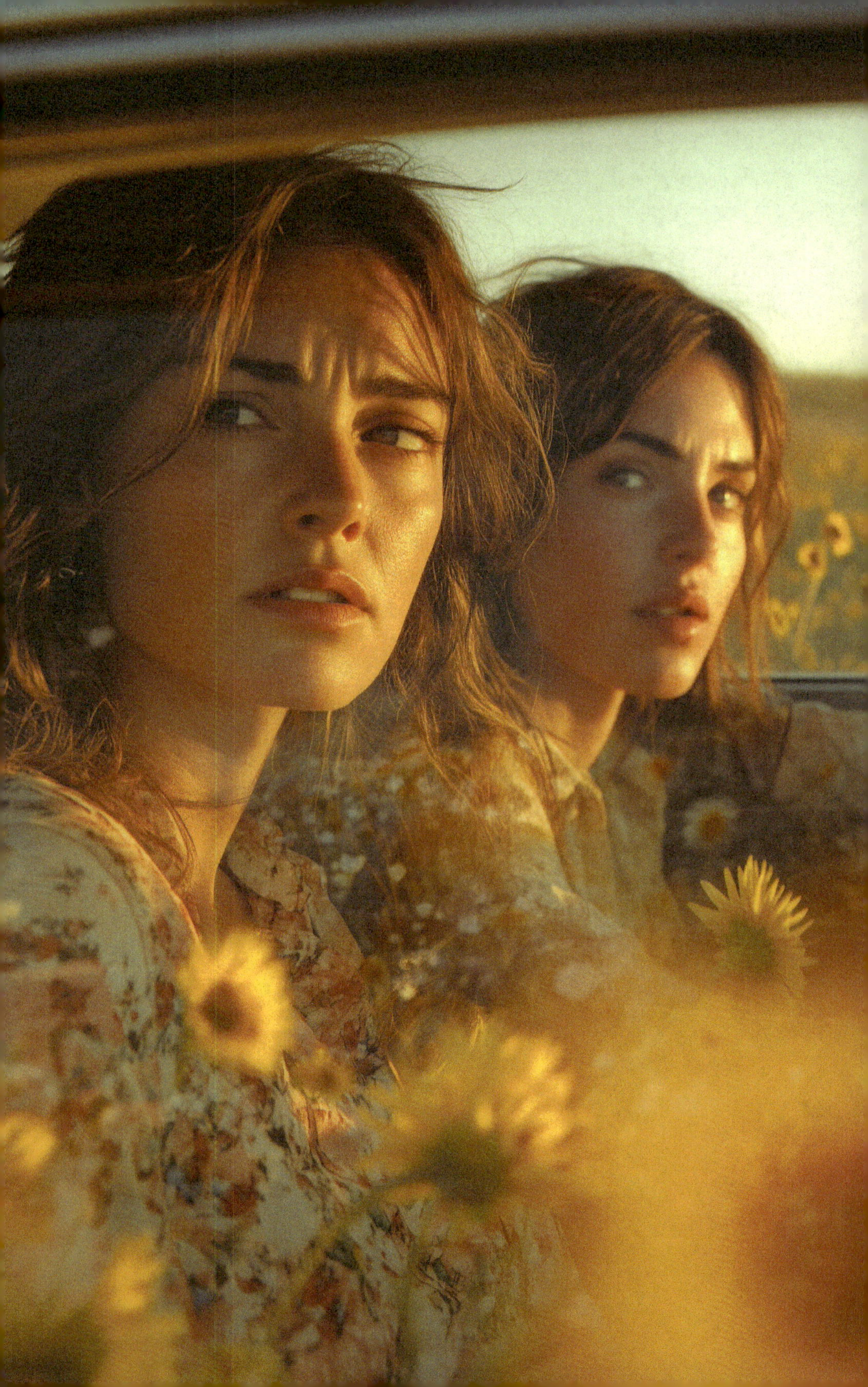

Sunflower Grin

Andrea was a flight attendant, always hopping between America and Europe. Between flights, she often took a week off to explore new places. It was during one such break in a city she had never visited that she heard whispers about Sunflower Grin—a woman with sunflower hair, a pale, almost ghostly face, giant black eyes, and a grin that never faded, never stopped mocking. They said she'd answer any question you asked her—but only once. After that, she'd never speak to you again. People said she could tell the future. And people tested that, spreading the story, turning it into a legend.

Andrea was intrigued. She had a week off, and she was in a city with nothing else to do. The legend led her to an old farm, a sunflower field that everyone in town had heard about. The taxi driver warned her to turn back, but Andrea didn't care. Nothing could stop her now.

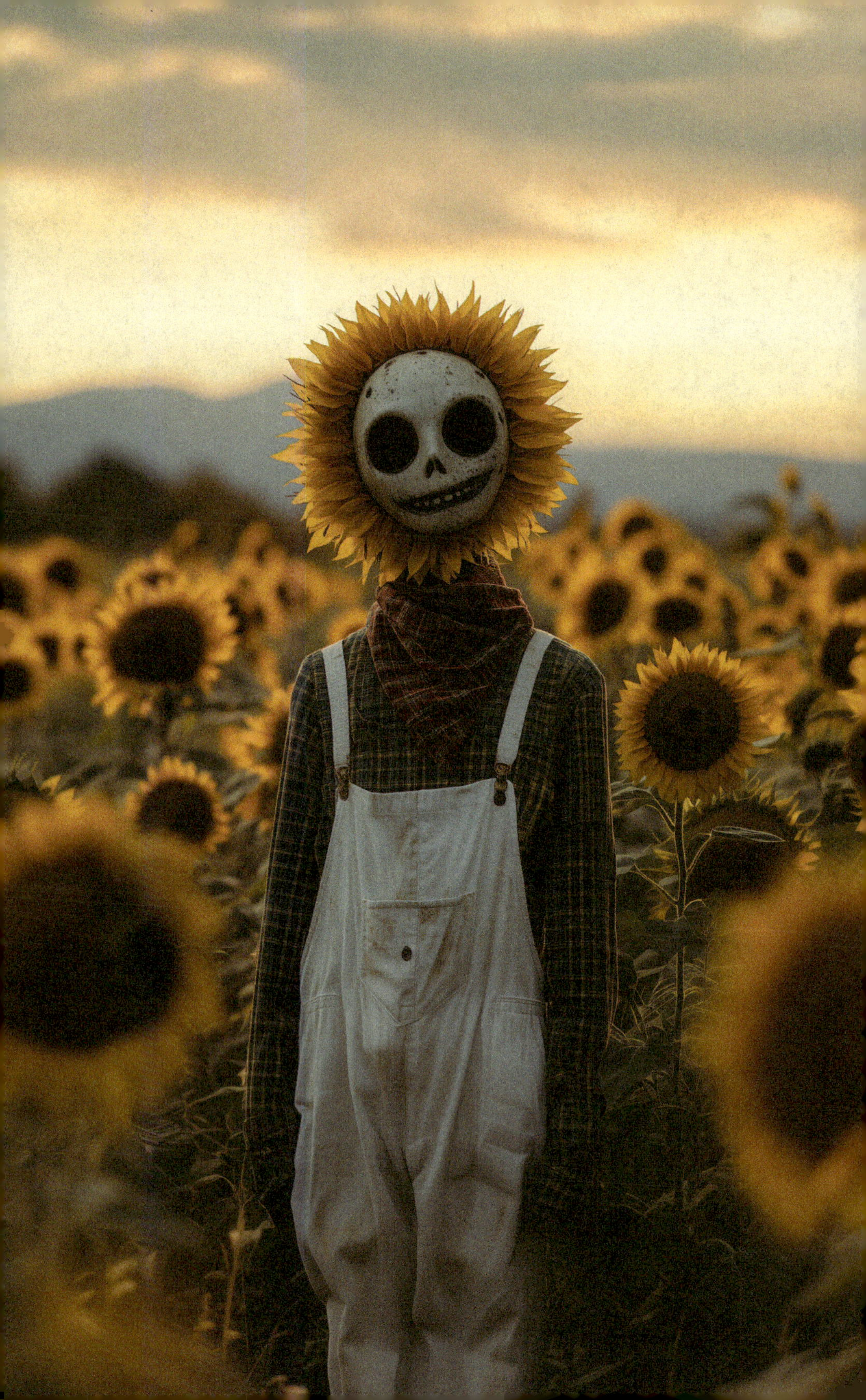

When she finally found Sunflower Grin, it was like stepping into another world. The woman stood there, impossibly thin, her movements unnaturally slow. She wore white overalls, a green plaid shirt, and a red neckerchief. Her head—no, her flower—was shaped like a sunflower, the large yellow petals stretching around her ghostly white face. Her eyes were deep pools of black—endless black. And that grin. That mocking, cold grin never left her face.

She bowed. Andrea felt her heart race. She had to ask her one question. The one question that would tell her the future. Andrea's voice trembled, but she forced herself to speak. "When will I die?"

Sunflower Grin paused, as if considering the question for too long. Then she leaned in, her black eyes gleaming with something like pity. "You'll die in eight years... in a car crash."

Andrea's heart stopped. The air went cold. She couldn't breathe. That moment—those words—felt like a curse, like a noose tightening around her neck. That night, she couldn't sleep. The thought of that car crash haunted her. No matter what she did—no matter where she went—the road would come for her. She couldn't escape it.

Years passed. Five years. Six. Seven. Then one day, the calendar flipped, and there was just one year left. Eight years. She was going to die in a car crash. No avoiding it. No way out.

But then, an idea crept into her mind. Maybe, just maybe, there was a way to change it. If she showed someone else,

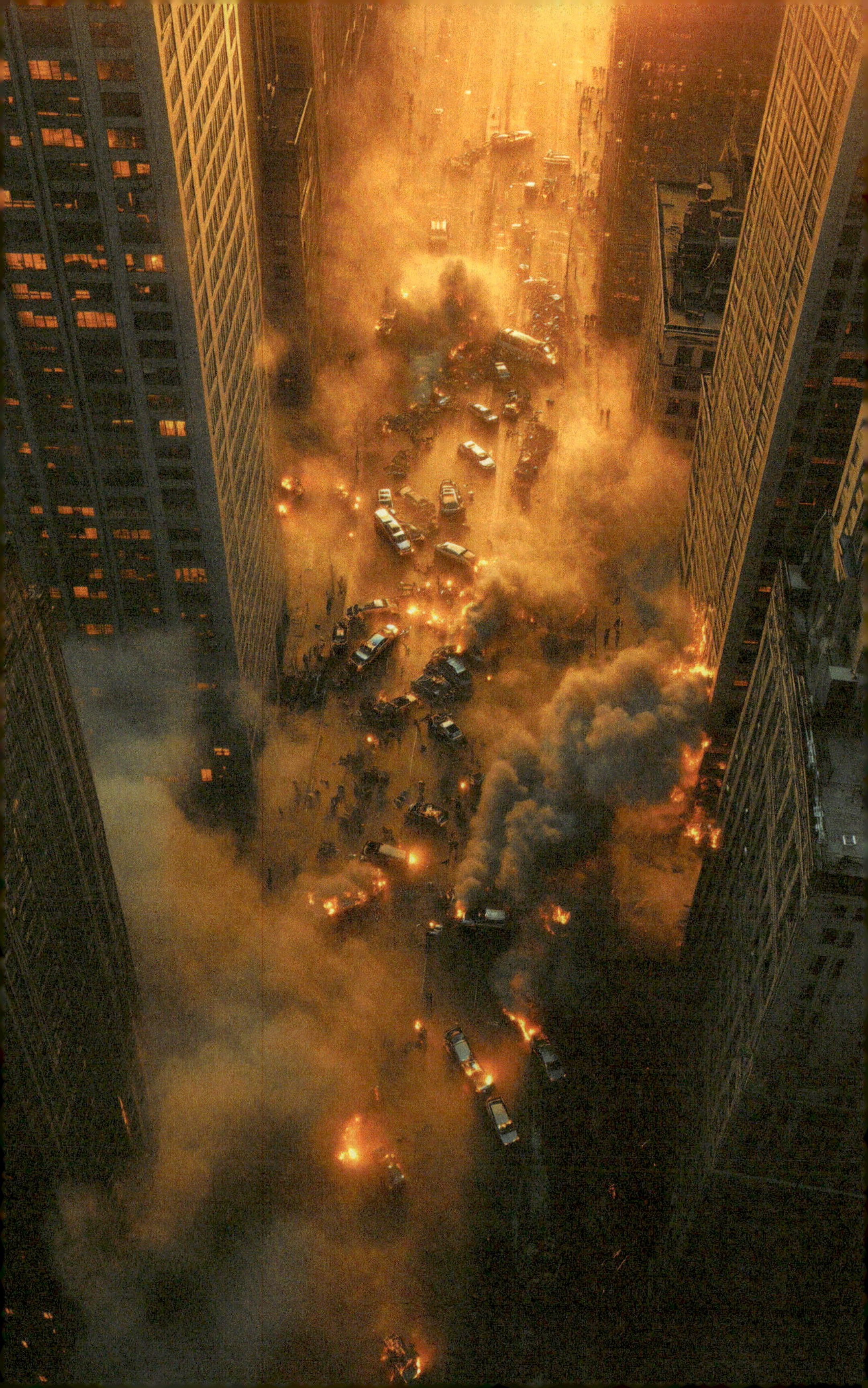

maybe they could change the outcome. She convinced a colleague to go on a road trip with her, spinning some story about Sunflower Grin being a myth—a legend, a trick—but deep down, Andrea knew it wasn't. She had to show her.

They drove to the sunflower field. Her colleague was terrified, but Andrea wouldn't let her back out. "Ask her," she urged. "Just ask her."

Finally, her colleague gave in, trembling. "What happens to Andrea in the afterlife?"

Sunflower Grin's grin stretched wider—if that was even possible. The words came slow, like they were being drawn out from deep within Andrea's soul. "In your next life, you will live the same number of years, but in reverse. You will see your mistakes before you make them, and only then will you live the original life again. But this time, you will fix them… or fail."

Andrea froze. The words echoed in her mind. Reverse? Play her life backward? Fix her mistakes? It sounded like a curse—a never-ending cycle of regret and repetition. But the way Sunflower Grin spoke, so casual, so detached—it made it feel all too real.

The drive back was silent. Andrea's colleague was visibly shaken, but Andrea? She couldn't stop thinking about what she'd just heard. The countdown loomed over her. Would she die on this road? The next? Was Sunflower Grin bluffing?

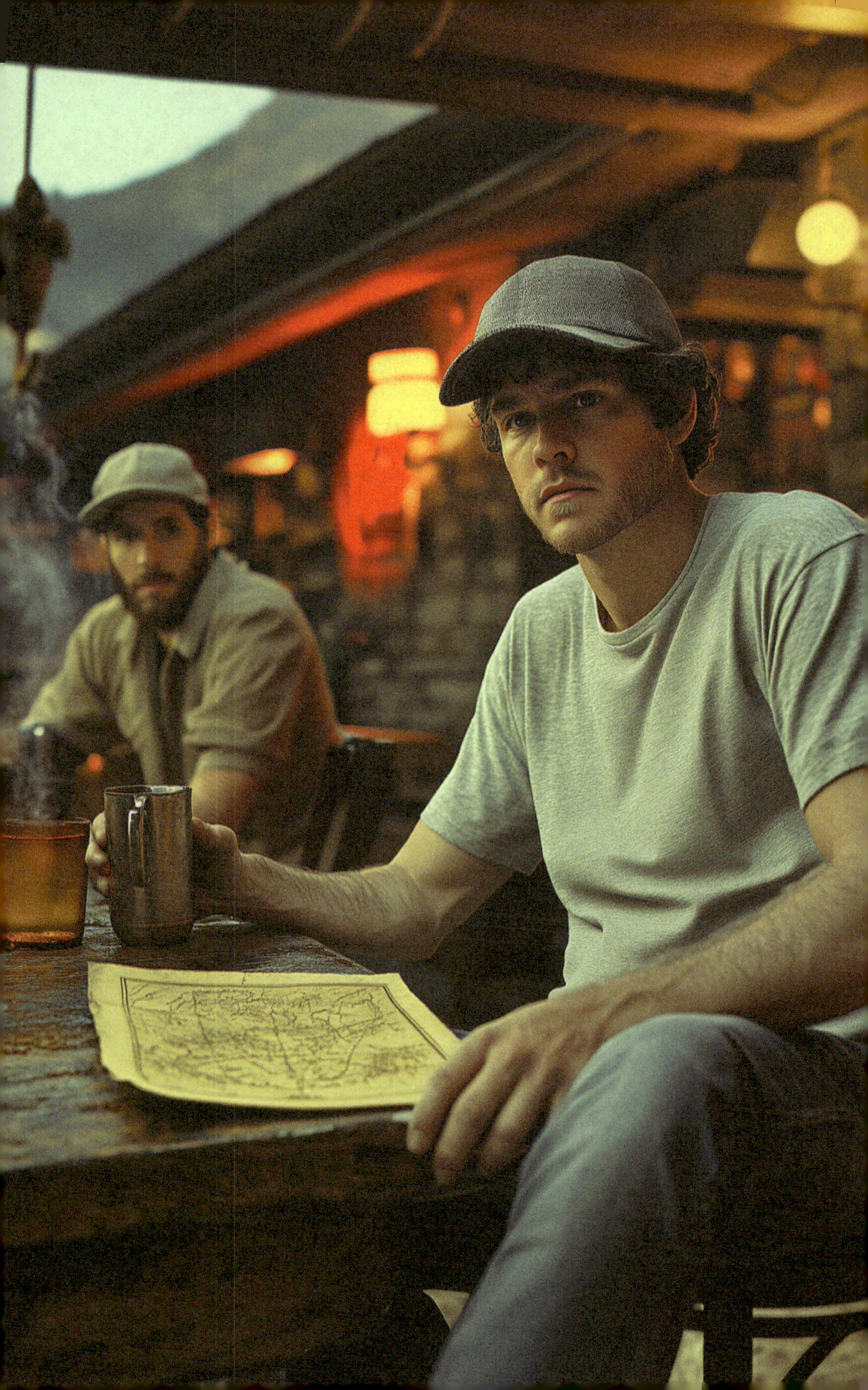

Canyon Crypt

Jaxon wasn't a man of principles. He was a landscaper, a bit of a fraud, and an opportunist when the moment struck. For a time, he had even been a pickpocket—though he hadn't stolen anything in over a year. But one night, while waiting for a blind date at his favorite bar—an old, cozy cottage made of weathered wood—a man approached him.

The stranger was around Jaxon's age, with a grey baseball cap pulled low over a scruffy beard. He wore a loose, beige shirt that looked too big for him, and his hands trembled as he dug into his pocket.

His voice was jittery, his words stumbling over each other as he pulled out a crumpled, yellowed piece of paper. "A treasure map," he whispered, eyes darting around the room, as if afraid someone might overhear. "Gems, coins, jewels…" He paused, his gaze unfocused. "It's all here. I can show you."

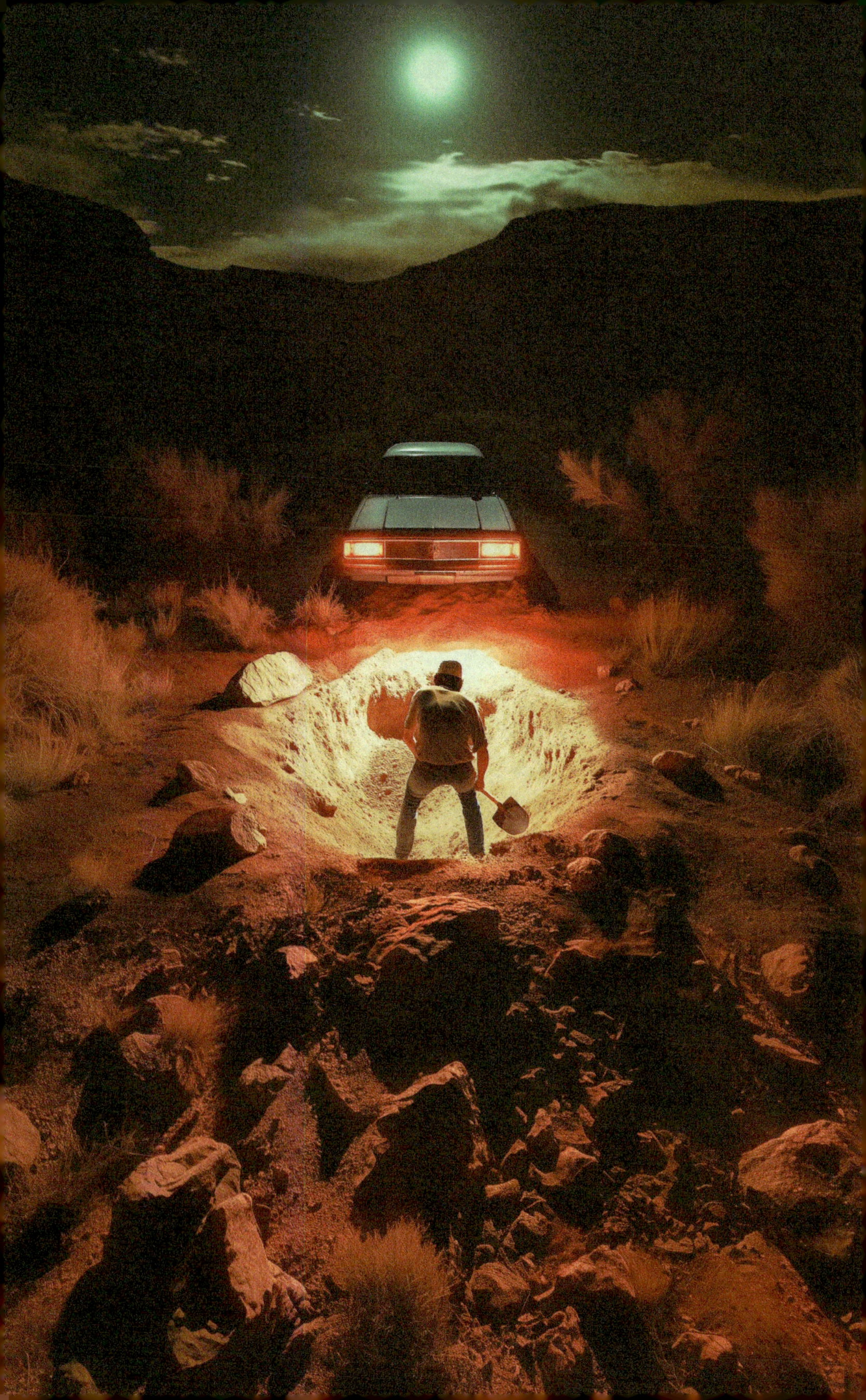

Jaxon was skeptical, but there was something strange about the man—nervous, but desperate. He didn't have time to fully process the situation before the man's phone rang, breaking the tension. The stranger practically lunged to answer it, almost forgetting about Jaxon and the map in his hands. With the man distracted, Jaxon saw his chance. Without hesitation, he pocketed the map and slipped away unnoticed.

Back in his car, Jaxon studied the map. Directions. Coordinates. A mark that told him to dig. Dig. The idea of treasure gnawed at him—gems, coins, jewels. His fingers trembled with anticipation as he grabbed a shovel, a pickaxe, and a rope from his house and sped off toward the canyon.

It took an hour to get there, and another hour searching before he found the red flag planted in the rock, marking the spot. He didn't waste time.

The pickaxe clanged against the earth, the shovel following in rhythm. His muscles ached with each strike, but the thought of fortune pushed him forward.

The hole deepened—ten feet, then twenty. By then, he tied the rope to his car bumper, making sure he had a way to climb out.

But after five hours of digging, the ground was still stubborn. Exhausted, Jaxon leaned against the hole's edge, his breath ragged. He let his eyes close, just for a moment.

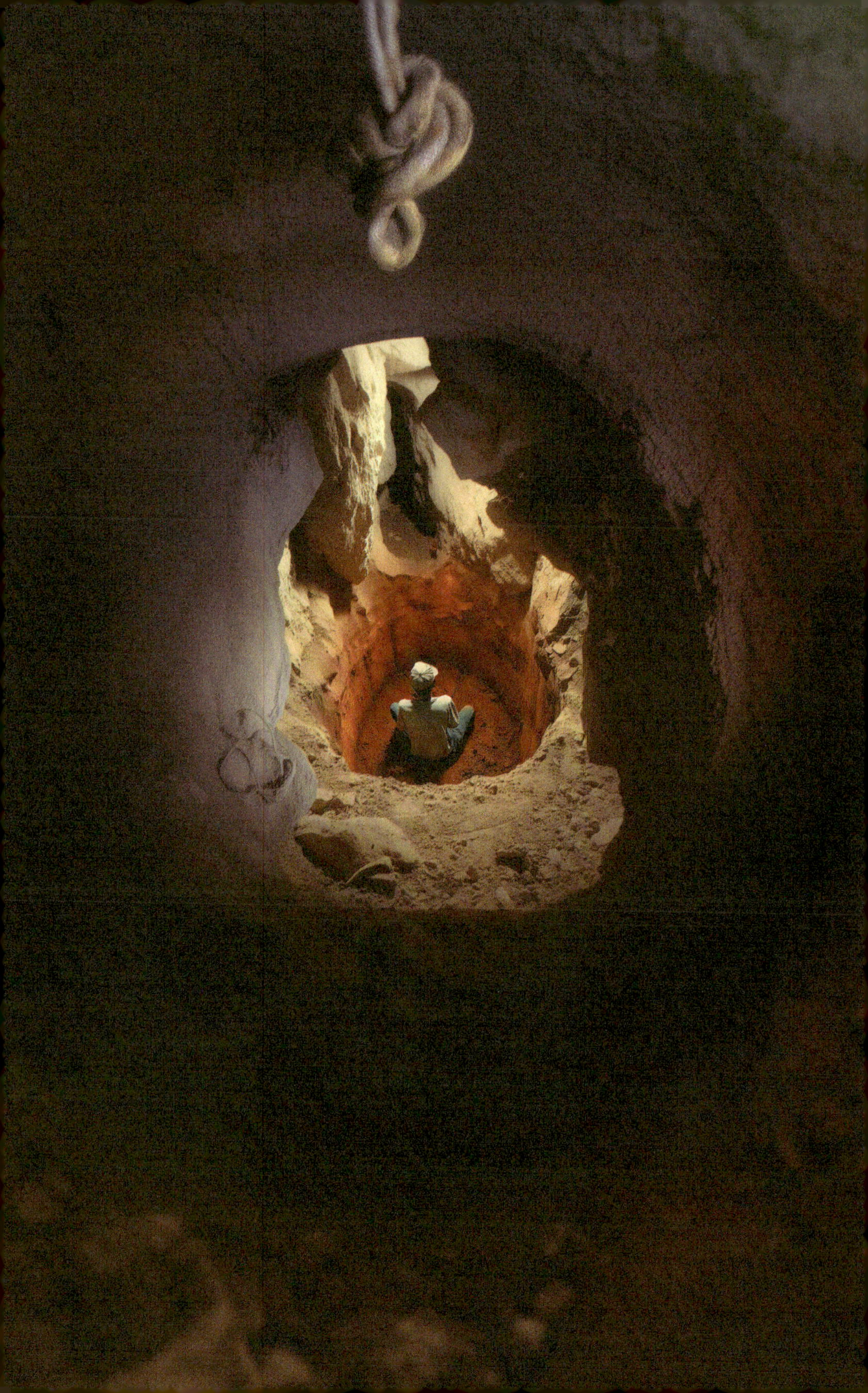

When he opened them again, the rope was out of reach. The bottom of it dangled tauntingly, ten feet above his head.

Panic surged through him.

He scrambled to the side of the hole, piling rocks beneath him, but they crumbled beneath his weight. He couldn't reach it. His heart pounded in his chest as the shadows closed in around him. He had no phone, no way to call for help. The only person who knew where he was was the strange man.

Would he come back?

Jaxon's thoughts spiraled. Why would he? To laugh at him?

Desperation clawed at him as he shouted, his voice echoing in the silence. But there was no answer.

He waited. Minutes turned to hours, and still, no one came. The rope remained just out of reach.

Jaxon was alone.

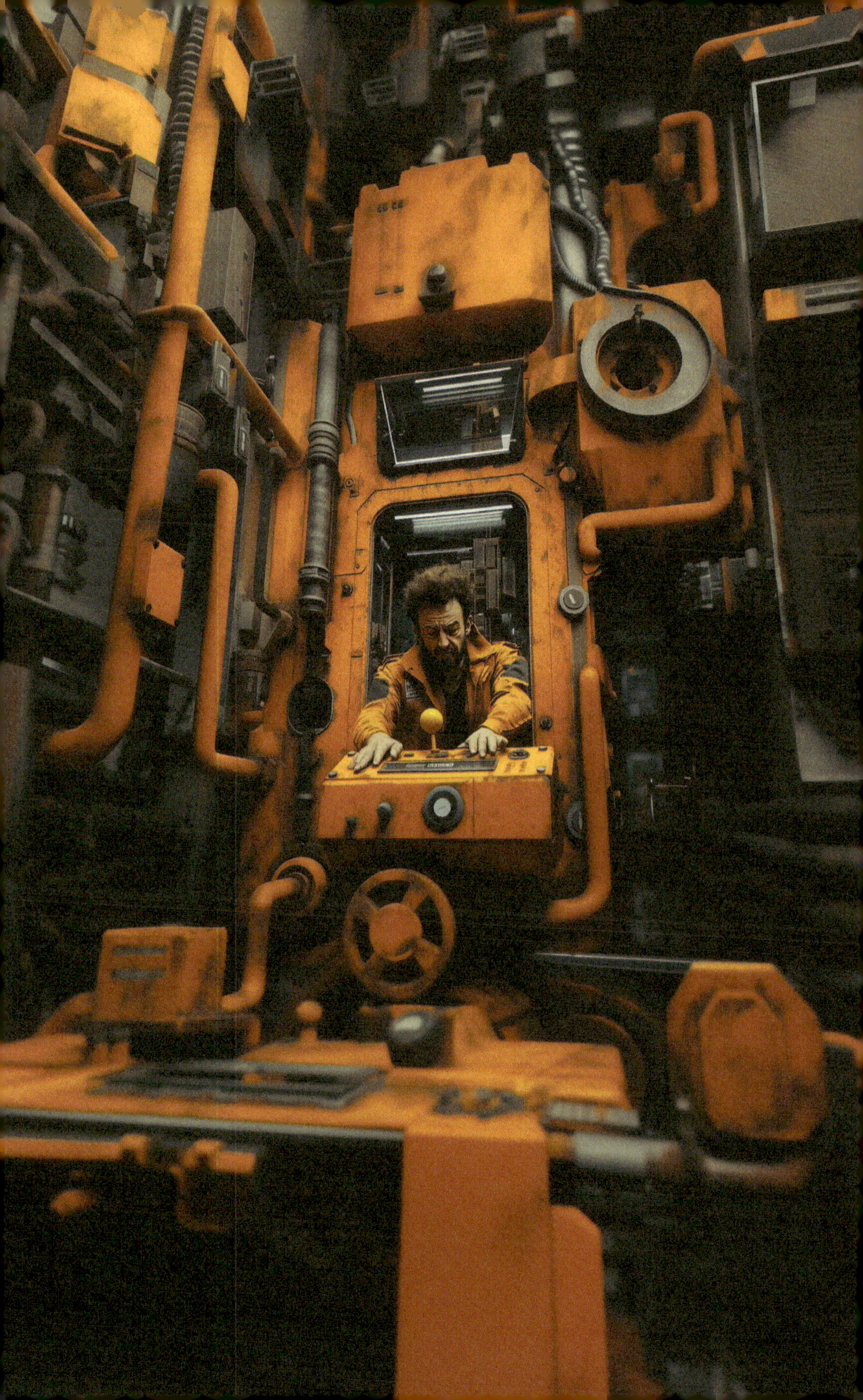

Bad Product

Jerry had been grinding through the graveyard shift at the same factory for two decades. The pay was lousy—a five-year drought without a raise—and his bills piled up. The factory was vast, a mechanical labyrinth that had quadrupled in size since he started. Its walls were a sickly orange, the same as his uniform. Everything in the factory was that color, like it had bled into every corner of his life.

As prices climbed, Jerry took on more hours, stretching each night shift longer until he was practically living in the factory. His world narrowed to repetitive motions—pushing buttons, pulling levers, flipping switches on a never-ending parade of broken machinery. Each click drilled deep into his mind until he couldn't stop himself. Jerry's compulsion to press buttons infected his life; he was drawn to them like magnets. Elevators were the worst—he couldn't resist pressing every button.

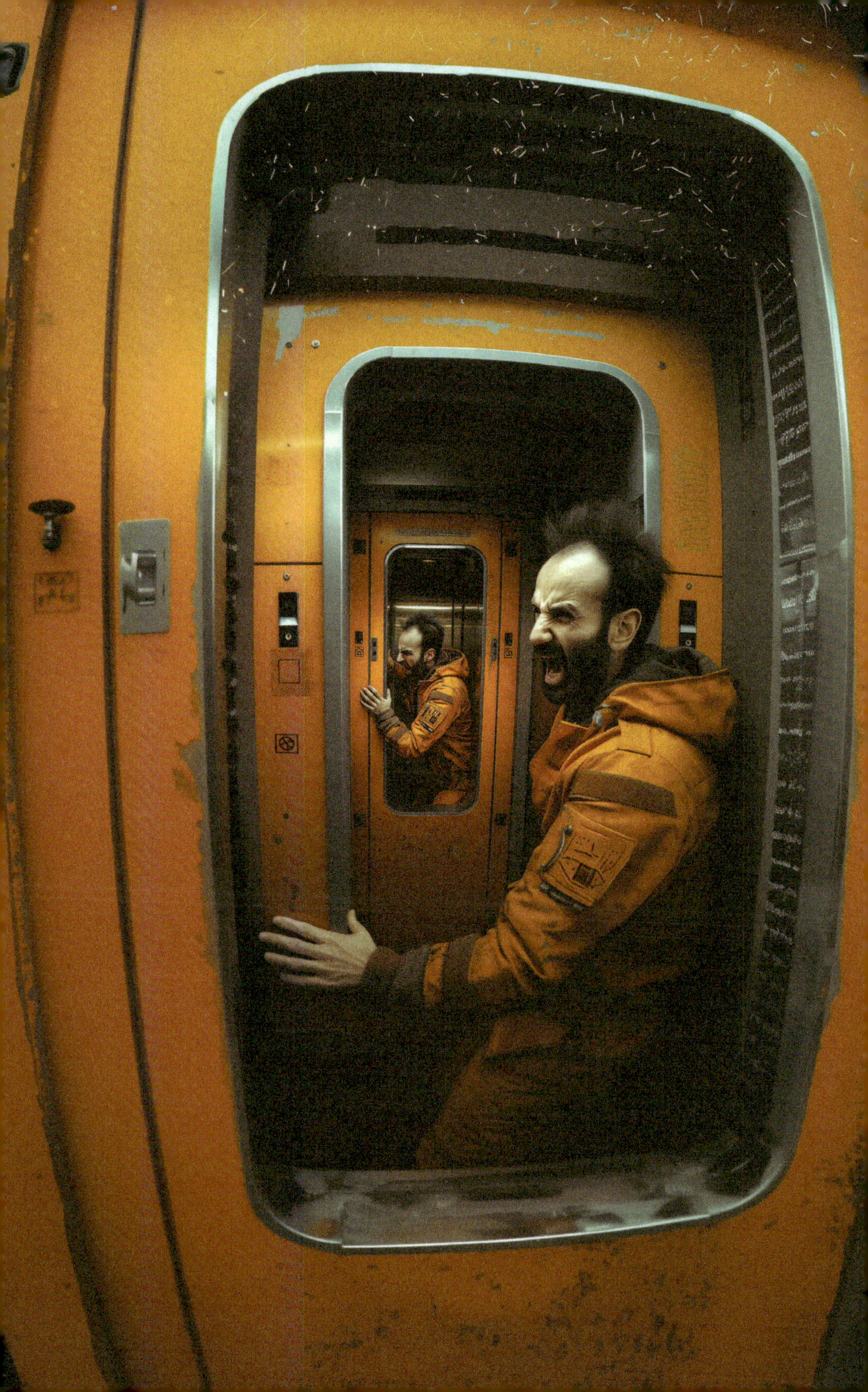

Then, one night, Jerry got a promotion. A single dollar raise to operate a new machine in a dark, deserted wing. The machine was colossal, surrounded by gears and pipes that hissed steam. His only tools were a worn joystick and a panel of buttons. No instructions. Just the strange console. Jerry's fingers itched. He began to press buttons in random sequences, flicking switches, gripping the joystick. The machine roared to life: gears churned, pistons pumped, steam hissed. It was hypnotic.

But then he saw it. A flash of orange out of the corner of his eye—a figure darting down the hallway. He caught a glimpse of a man in an orange coat, but he was gone. He chased after the stranger, shouting, but the corridors were empty, filled only with the hum of machines. He went back to the machine, heart racing, but couldn't shake the feeling that he wasn't alone.

As days passed, the machine consumed Jerry's mind. He grew obsessed, convinced he was close to understanding it. Occasionally, he heard footsteps, a distant scream, but when he searched, he found nothing. The vast, silent halls seemed to stretch on forever.

Finally, one night, everything clicked. A hidden panel in the machine room slid open, revealing a metallic chamber—a small cabin with a glass window. Jerry climbed inside and faced a new array of buttons. Thirty-six of them. He pressed each one, feeling a rush with every click. A door opened to another cabin. Then another. The cabins became a maze—

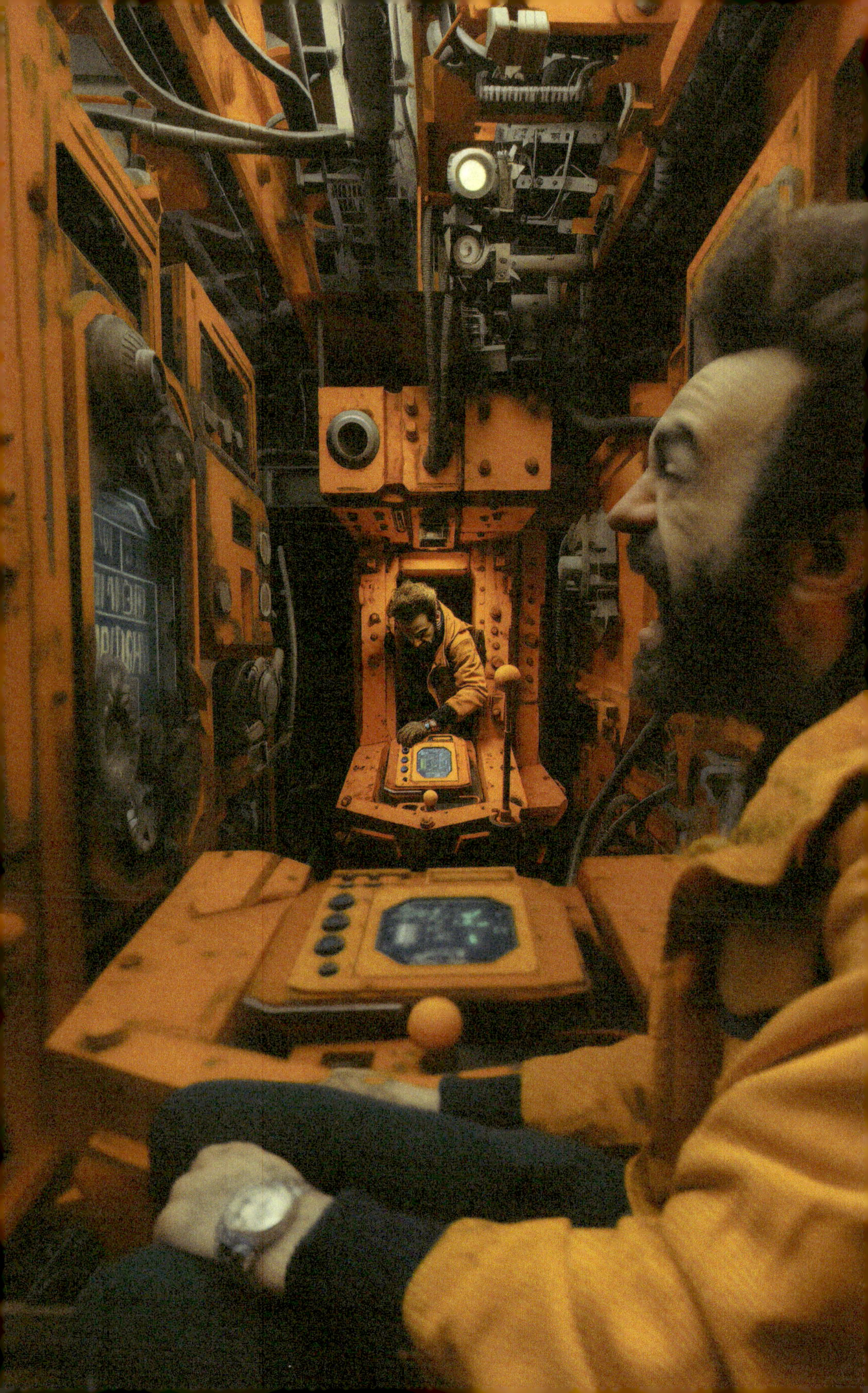

endless metal chambers connected by hidden doors. He moved deeper, the walls closing in, the air growing colder. He couldn't tell where he'd come from, couldn't remember how to go back. Then he saw him—the man in the orange coat. No, not just any man... him, Jerry. The same face, the same hollow eyes. The man bolted, and Jerry chased him, through the maze, through door after door, each leading deeper. Hours blurred together, or was it days? Each chamber looked the same. There were no clocks, no light except the dull factory glow. Jerry's breath hitched as he ran, sweat pouring down his face. He'd lost count of the doors, the buttons. The walls were closing in.

He stumbled into a new section of the maze. This wasn't just metal—it was the guts of a machine, corridors of exposed wires, gears spinning overhead, steam hissing from pipes. And he wasn't alone. More figures in orange coats moved in the shadows. They turned to face him, and he saw his own eyes staring back. Dozens of Jerrys, faces twisted with despair, all trapped in this hell. They muttered to him in broken voices, "There's no way out. We've tried... we've all tried..." Each had been here for years, driven mad by the same machine, lost in the same maze. Their faces mirrored his terror, reflecting the fate that awaited him.

Jerry stumbled back, heart pounding, but there was no way out. The machine pulsed around him, gears turning, whispering secrets he couldn't understand. He was one of them now—just another cog in a machine that never stopped turning.

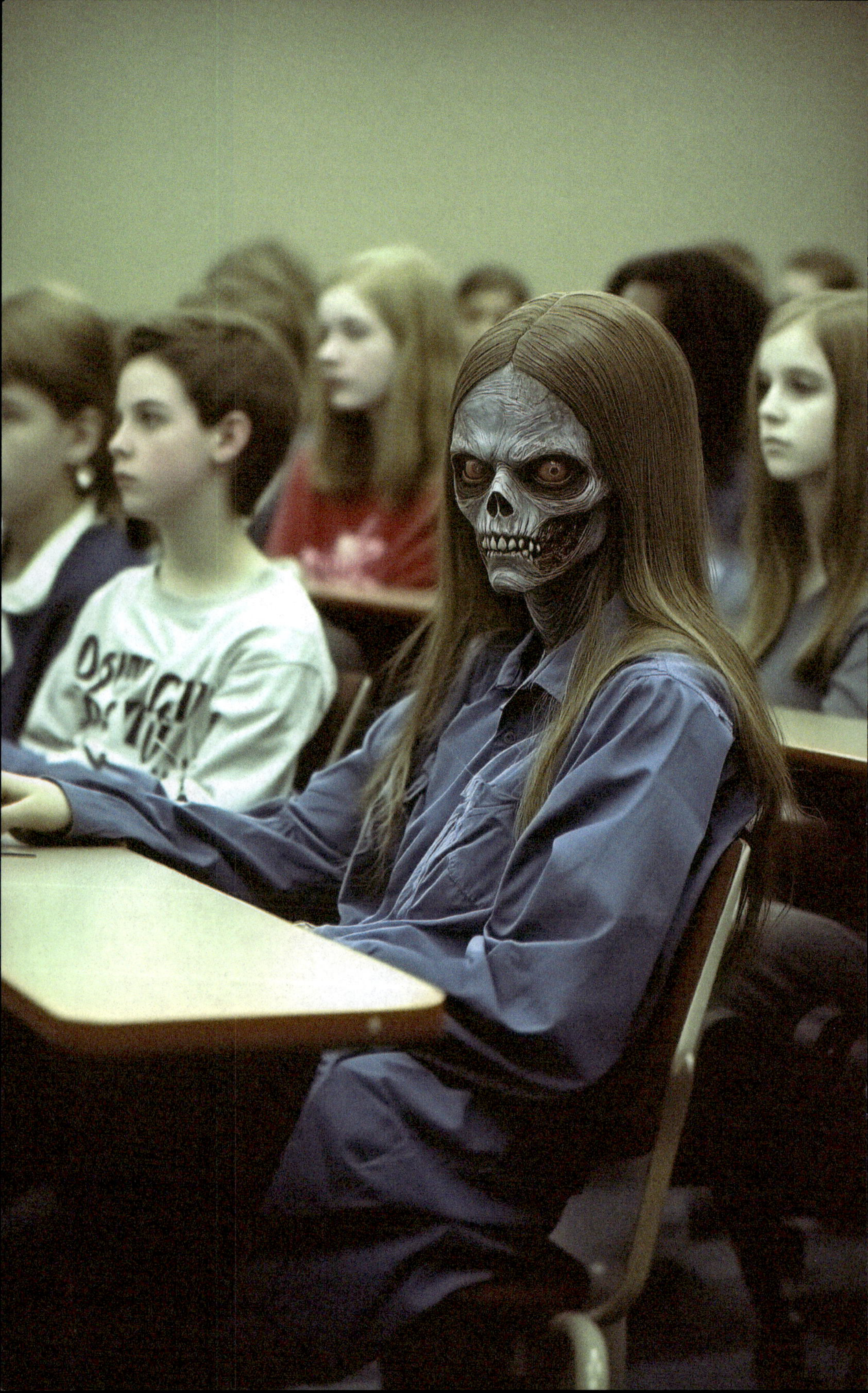

Strange Student

It was Mason's first day of 8th grade when he encountered her—the girl who seemed to exist just for him. She entered as the bell rang, her presence unsettling. Her face was grey, wrinkled, almost alien, and her eyes were dark, hollow—like something long dead. She didn't look at anyone, not even the teacher, but when Mason's gaze met hers, a cold terror gripped him. It felt as though she was studying him, waiting.

The other students chattered on, oblivious, but Mason couldn't tear his eyes away. Her stare held him in place, paralyzing him with fear. His heart thudded painfully in his chest, and every time he tried to look away, his eyes snapped back to hers, as though drawn by some unseen force.

Finally, overwhelmed, Mason asked to use the bathroom. The teacher hardly seemed to notice as he stumbled out of the room, his legs trembling.

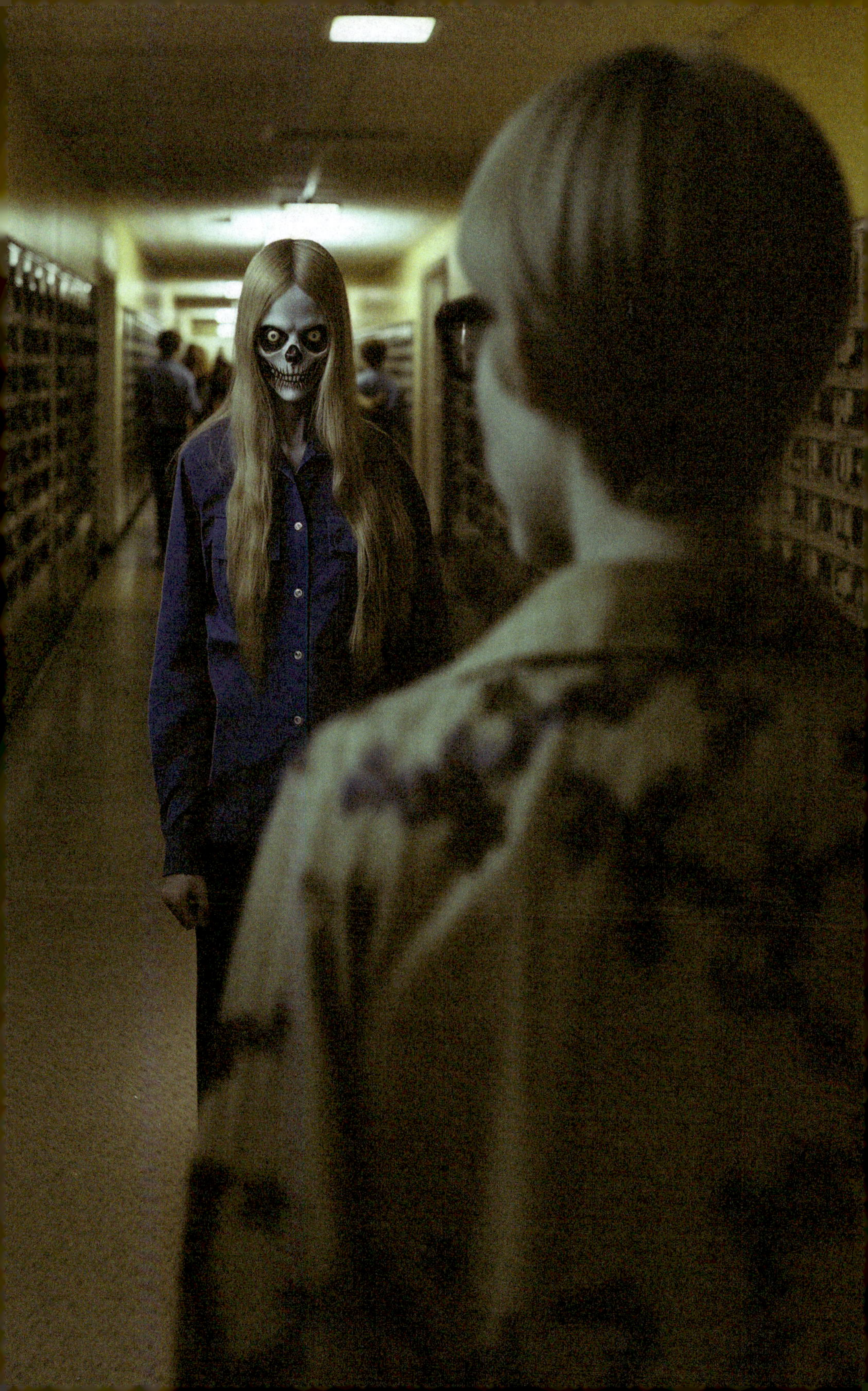

He needed air. As he reached his locker, there she was again. Her movements were slow, deliberate, as though she knew exactly where she was going. Mason followed, against his better judgment.

Then she turned.

"Why are you following me?" Her voice was disturbingly calm, too normal for someone who looked like her. Yet something about it made his skin crawl.

Mason froze, his pulse quickening. Was this some kind of hallucination?

"Stop following me," she said, her voice flat and knowing, "or I'll remind you what you are."

Her words sent a shiver down his spine. He turned quickly, but the unease gnawing at him wouldn't let go. He veered down three hallways, hoping to lose her. But when he rounded the next corner, she was there again, slipping into the emergency stairway.

His heart raced. He followed her, descending quickly. At the bottom, a door slammed shut behind her. Mason slipped through just before it closed.

The mechanical room was dim, filled with the hum of old boilers and air systems. Rust and oil hung in the air, the place a maze of steel and shadows. Mason's eyes scanned the misty space, searching for her.

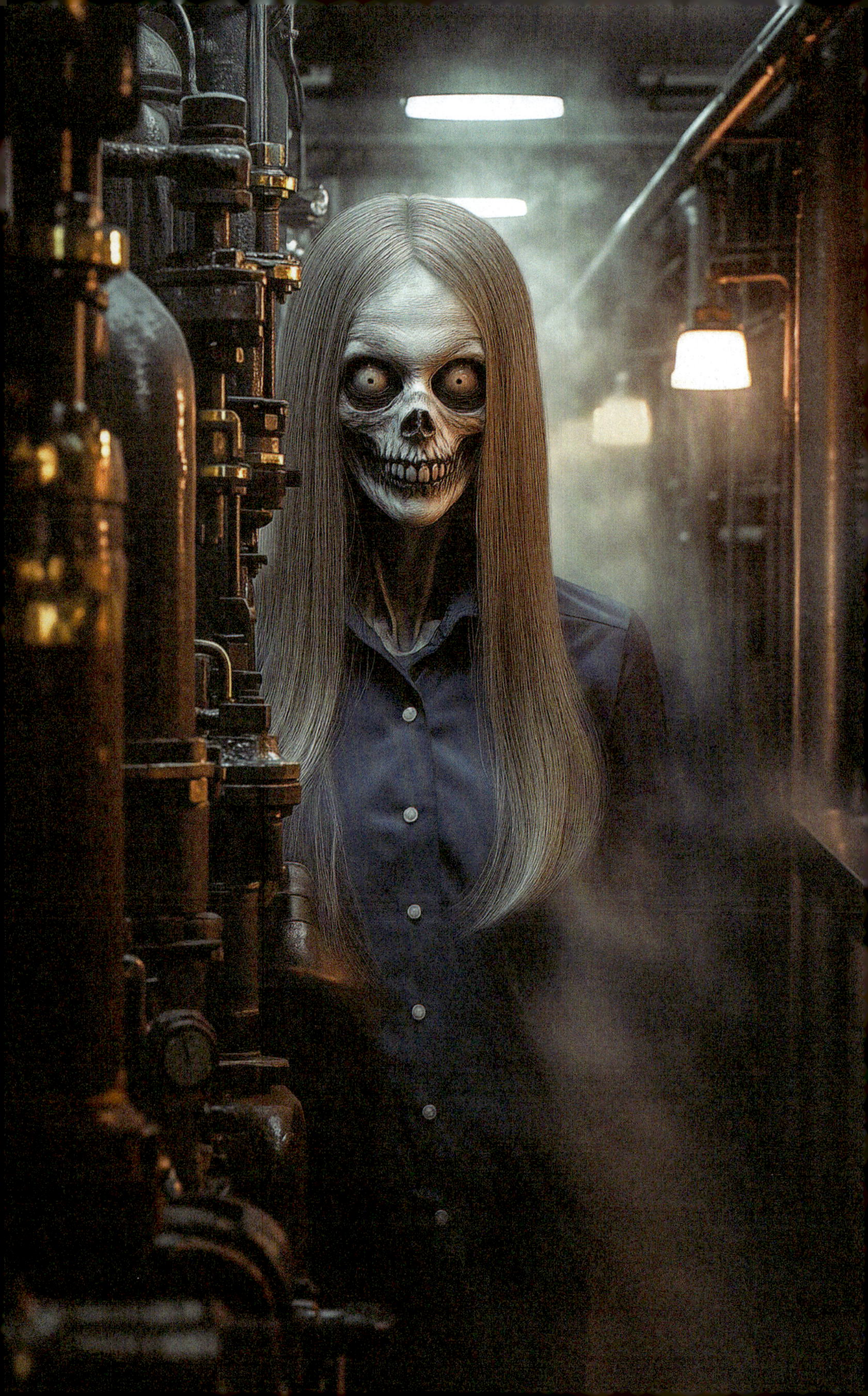

Then, through the steam, he saw her again.

Her face was more twisted now—grey skin stretched tight, her eyes deeper, darker. Her smile was wrong—unnaturally wide, like something long dead.

"You're one of us now," she whispered, her voice chillingly calm. "A ghost. You haunt this school, reliving your first day over and over. You forget each time. This school burned down 16 years ago. We're all trapped."

Mason's heart froze in his chest. "What... are you talking about?"

Before he could speak, she vanished into the mist.

The world tilted, the room spinning around him. His vision blurred, and in the blink of an eye, everything was gone.

When Mason opened his eyes again, he was back in the classroom. The students were laughing, talking. The strange girl was nowhere to be seen.

A sinking dread filled him. He couldn't remember anything—nothing at all. It was as if it had never happened.

As the bell rang again, Mason sat quietly, the weight of his forgotten existence pressing down on him. A ghost, forever lost in time.

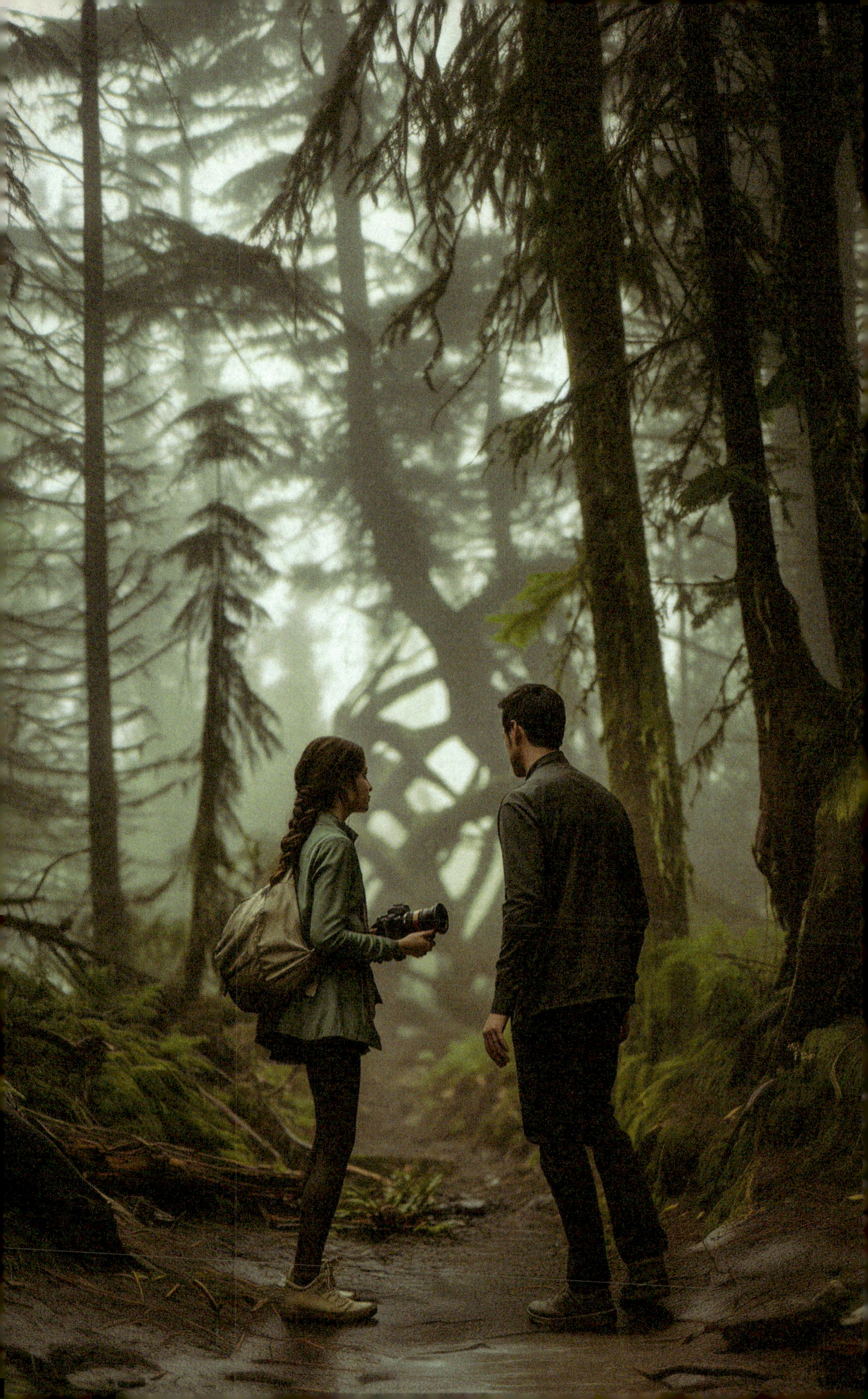

Tree Hunter

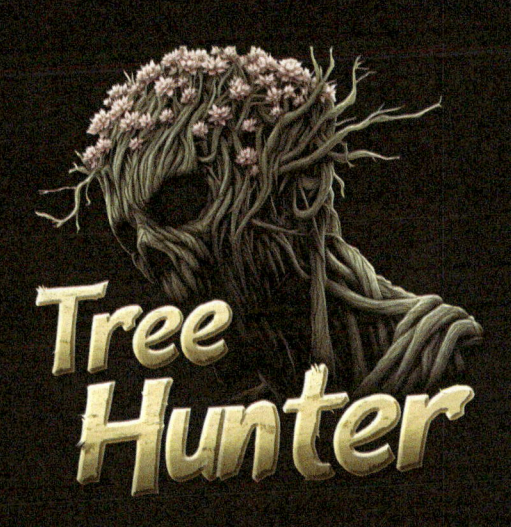

Madison never understood Ethan's obsession with cryptids. He chased myths, but the Fleshtree? This felt different—dangerous. He described it as a towering, humanoid creature made of twisted roots, vines, and grotesque flowers. It captured anything in its path, dragging them into the forest where they vanished forever. Madison didn't believe it, of course. But when Ethan asked her to film his investigation, how could she say no?

They ventured deeper into the woods, the trees growing taller, the air growing colder. The wind carried a strange hum. Madison kept the camera trained on Ethan as he rambled about the Fleshtree, his eyes wild with excitement. He didn't seem to notice, or didn't care, how much his talk unsettled her. She was starting to think this wasn't about finding truth, but about proving something—something she wasn't sure she wanted to know.

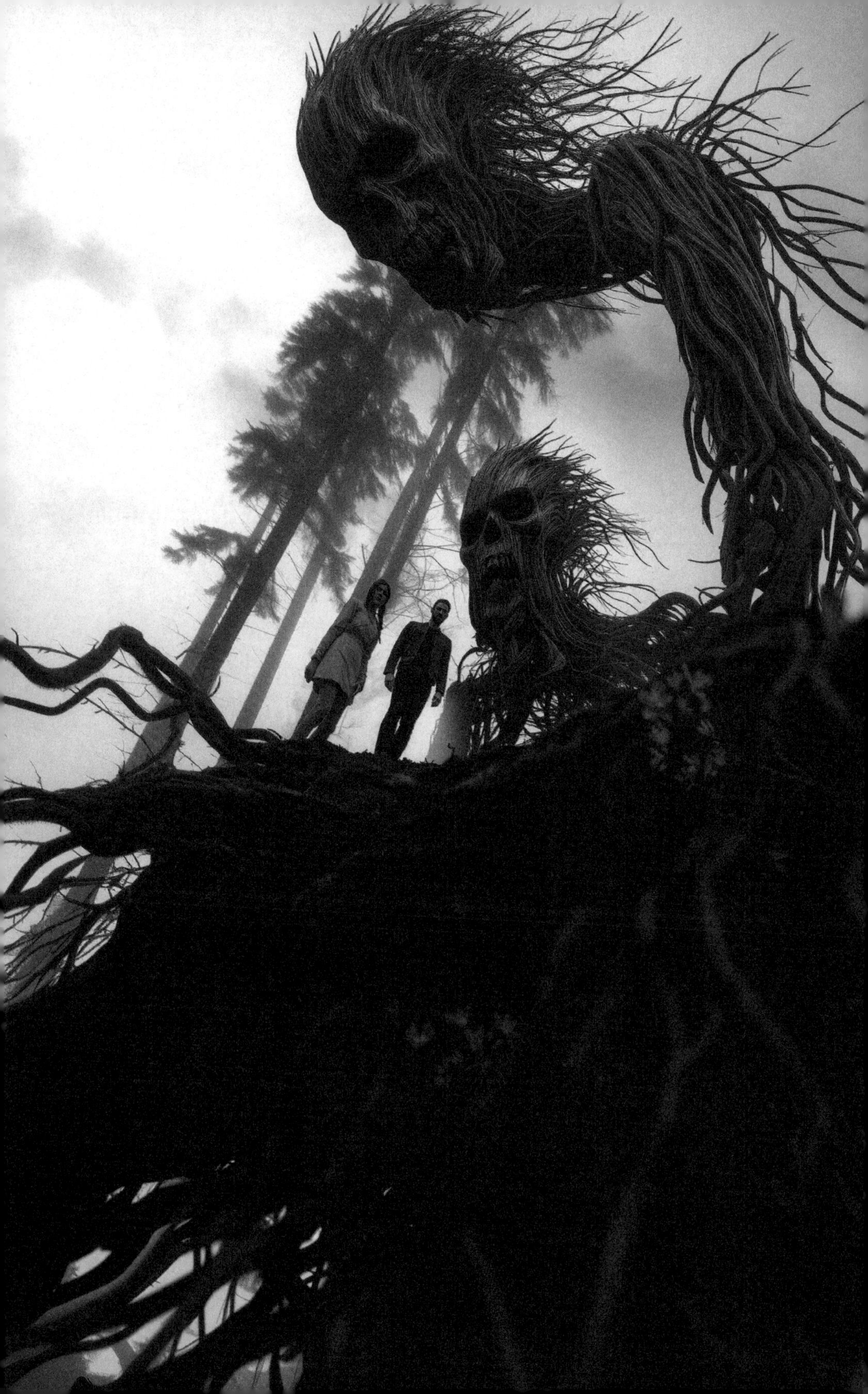

"There's something about the disappearances," Ethan said, his voice almost a whisper as he looked up at the darkening sky. "Some say the Fleshtree turns them into tree-like marks, forever frozen in wood. Makes you wonder…"

Madison shivered. "You really think it's real?"

Ethan didn't answer, lost in his thoughts. As the sun dipped behind the trees, the atmosphere thickened. The forest felt alive in a way she couldn't explain. The shadows seemed deeper, the air colder. Madison kept filming, but her mind was drifting, wondering why she was still here, following Ethan through the growing darkness. Why was he so desperate to prove the existence of something so terrifying?

He lit another cigarette, the smoke swirling around him before he flicked it carelessly onto the ground. Madison scowled and crushed it beneath her boot.

"Ethan, you're going to start a fire," she snapped.

He didn't even look at her. "Chill out. You always freak out about stuff."

Tension thickened between them, more than just the cryptids now. It was something else—something unspoken, unresolved. Madison had been growing frustrated with him for days, but neither of them ever said it out loud.

Then, without warning, the ground beneath them trembled.

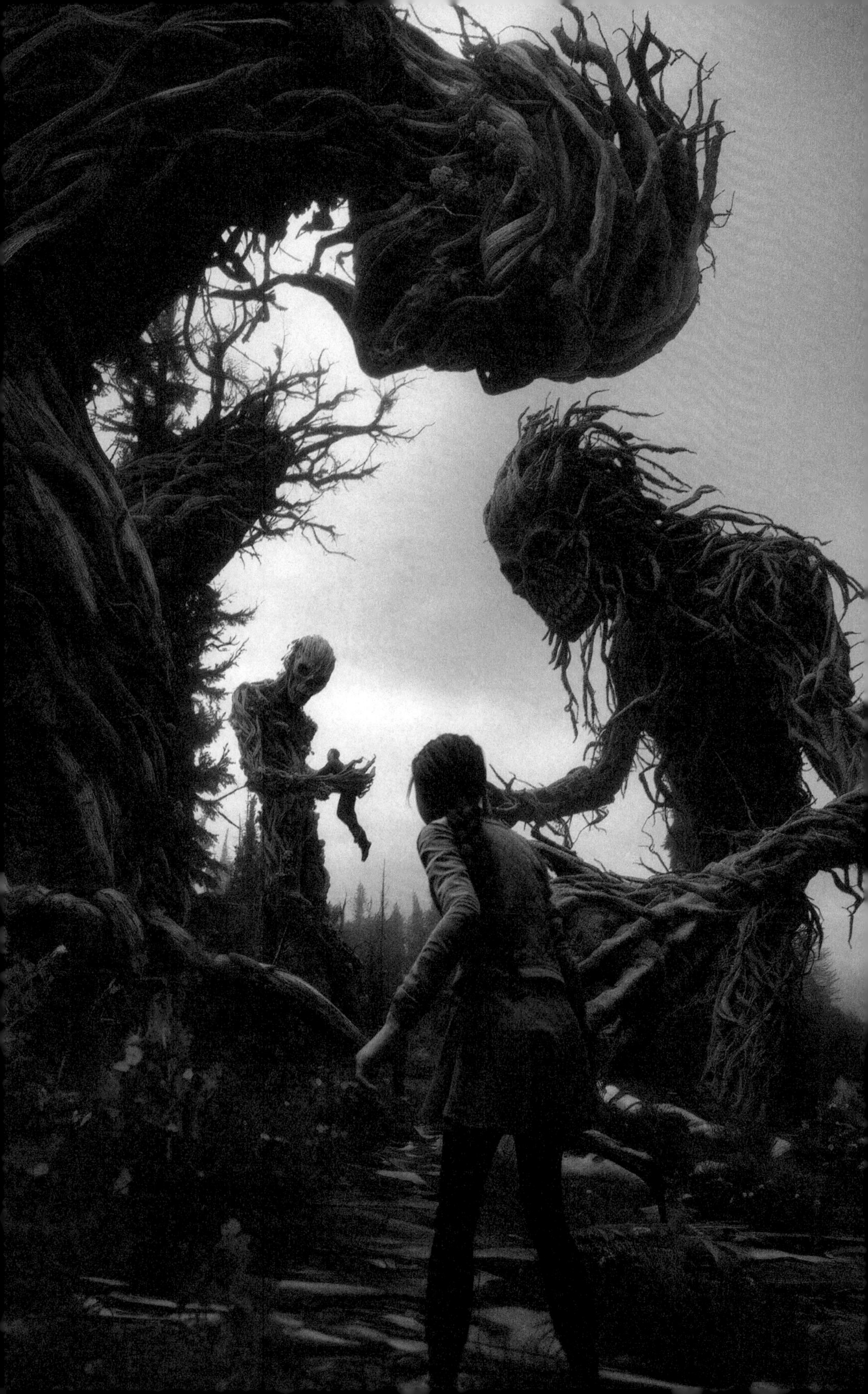

Madison froze. Ethan spun around, confused, as a crack echoed through the trees. From the earth, grotesque shapes began to rise. Twisted figures, their bark-like skin covered in pale, sickly pink flowers, emerged from the soil. The Fleshtrees.

Ethan gasped, taking a step back, but before he could react, a thick root shot out, coiling around his leg. He screamed as the vine dragged him toward one of the creatures. His skin twisted into bark, his body contorted grotesquely as the Fleshtree devoured him, his cries fading into an awful, gurgling silence.

Madison's breath caught in her throat. She didn't think—she ran.

The trees didn't chase her. They didn't need to. They were content with their prize.

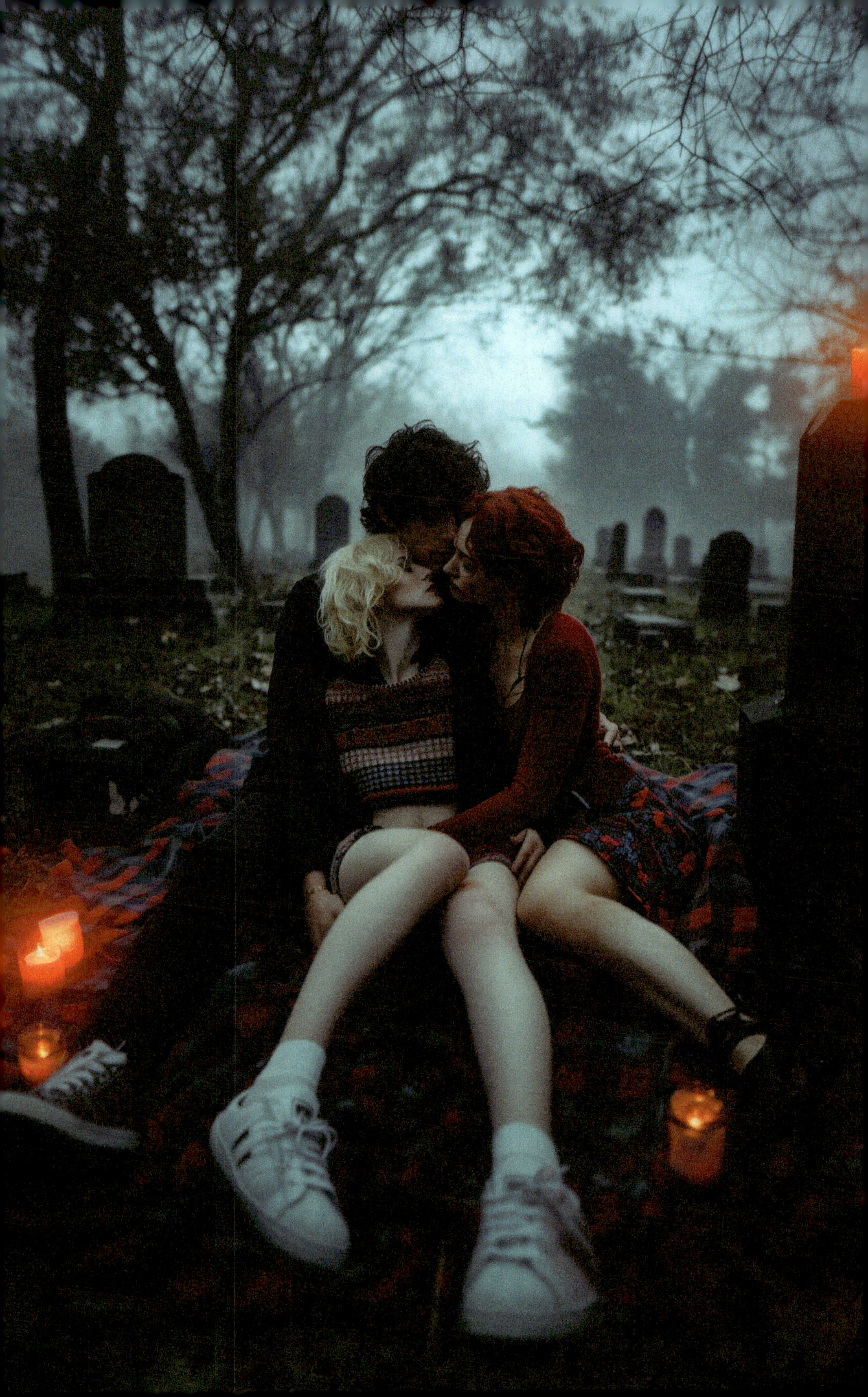

Graveyard Triad

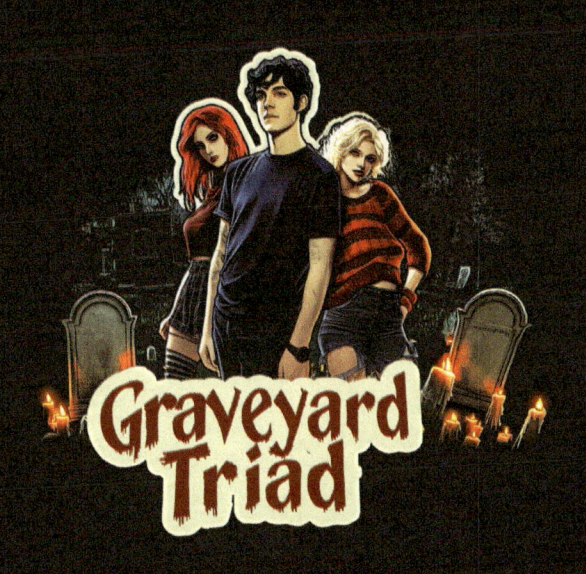

Stewart led a romantic triad that had blossomed three months earlier. He and his girlfriend, Kerrigan, had met Jenna at a Halloween party, and their connection grew until they became a trio. Their symbol was a blue rose, one that had mysteriously appeared in Stewart and Kerrigan's garden. They carried it always: Kerrigan in her hair, Stewart in his blazer pocket, and Jenna on her purse. The rose symbolized their unity—three equal parts of one love. It was a reminder that neglect or exclusion would fracture their bond, and so they nurtured their triad carefully.

One night, they planned a sensual picnic at an abandoned cemetery. The graveyard, overgrown with wild grass and crumbling tombstones, matched their taste for the macabre. The trio laughed, played, and indulged in Stewart's favorite game—a twisted version of hide-and-seek. The thrill of temporary separation stirred longing and jealousy, feelings they found tantalizing in their unity. Yet, as they ventured near the woods, an unsettling chill settled over the graveyard.

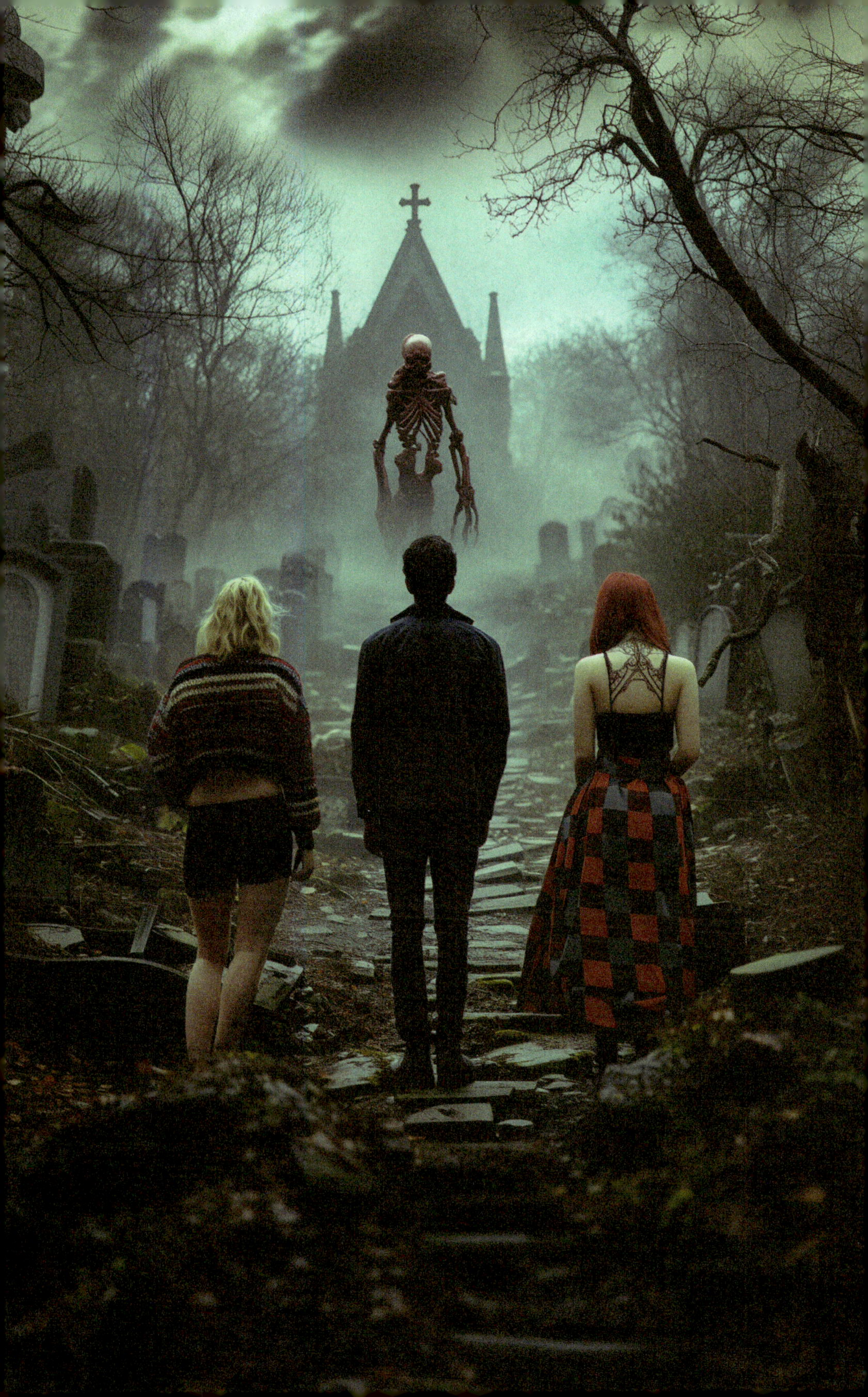

Kerrigan noticed cracks forming along the mausoleum's weathered surface, like veins creeping across its stone. Jenna swore she heard whispers beneath the wind. Stewart dismissed it as their imaginations, but the unease lingered. When the sun dipped below the horizon, the shadows stretched unnaturally long, and the air grew oppressive.

Their passions ignited as the twilight deepened, their careless laughter echoing through the tombs. But as their intimacy spilled across an ancient grave, the ground trembled violently. The mausoleum groaned, and from its shattered door emerged a 20-foot skeleton. It stood motionless, a towering figure of bone silhouetted against the moonlight.

"What do you want?" Stewart called, his voice steady despite the terror creeping into his chest. The skeleton didn't answer. Its hollow sockets seemed to see through them, waiting, judging.

Fear gripped them as they tried to flee. Yet, every path through the woods twisted back to the mausoleum. The cemetery stretched endlessly, a labyrinth of gravestones and shadows that defied logic. Exhausted and frantic, they regrouped before the mausoleum. Jenna, clutching her rose, stepped forward. "Why won't you let us go?" she demanded. The skeleton remained silent.

Kerrigan, trembling, asked, "How can we leave?"

At last, the skeleton spoke, its voice like grinding stone: "Two can leave. One stays."

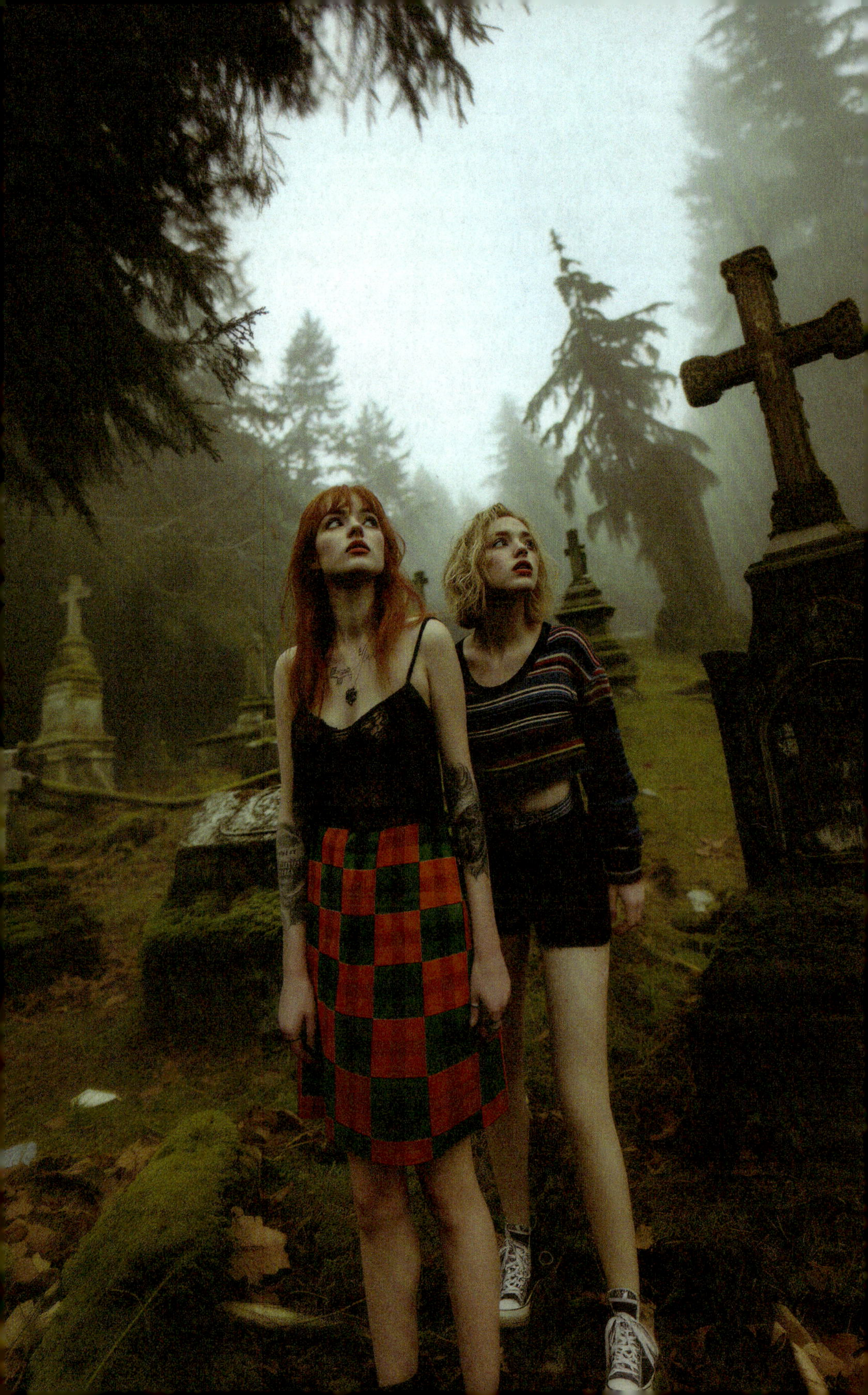

The words echoed in the night, cold and final. Stewart tried to guide Kerrigan and Jenna back into the woods, but every path led them in circles. The graveyard seemed to mock their unity, fraying the bond they had cherished so deeply. Jenna's fear turned to anger, Kerrigan's to tears. Stewart felt the weight of their trust, his love for both pulling him in opposite directions.

Finally, he stepped forward. "Take me," he said, his voice steady. "Let them go."

Without a word, the skeleton turned and entered the mausoleum. Stewart followed, his shadow disappearing into the crypt. The heavy stone door groaned shut behind him. The forest released Kerrigan and Jenna at last, and they stumbled to their car, hollow with grief.

From then on, Kerrigan and Jenna lived as a couple, bound by sorrow and gratitude. Their blue roses faded quickly after Stewart's disappearance, the once vibrant petals turning brittle and gray. Every year, they returned to the cemetery's edge, leaving a single fresh blue rose at the mausoleum gate—a token of love and loss. Yet they never ventured further, haunted by the memory of the skeleton's decree.

The blue rose remained their bittersweet reminder—a symbol of a bond once complete, now fractured. Though they left the cemetery together, the weight of Stewart's sacrifice lingered, casting its shadow over their lives and love.

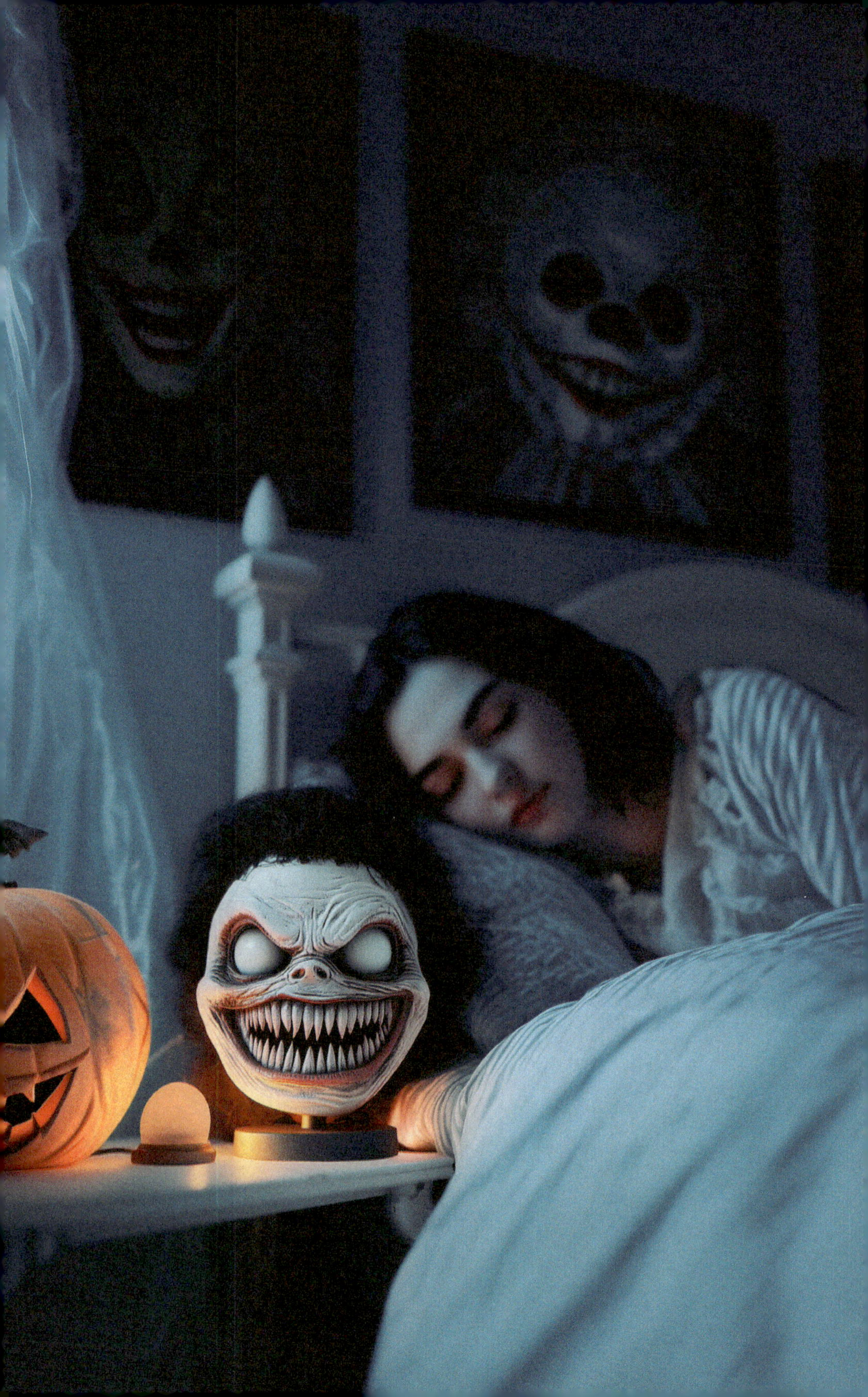

Mister Midnight

It was the night before Halloween, October 30th, when Avery found a package on her doorstep. Inside was a grotesque bobblehead—Mister Midnight, the infamous figure from a popular creepypasta. Its sharp-toothed grin, hollow white eyes, and wild, frizzy hair made it look disturbingly alive. Avery was more intrigued than scared. She loved creepypasta. Was it a trick? Or a treat?

Curiosity gnawed at her as she set the bobblehead on her bedside table. Who would send her this? And why?

Avery climbed into bed, turning on her favorite Mister Midnight podcast. The familiar voice filled the room, soothing her as she drifted toward sleep. But tonight, something felt off. The air around her thickened, as though the room itself was holding its breath.

Her eyes fluttered shut.

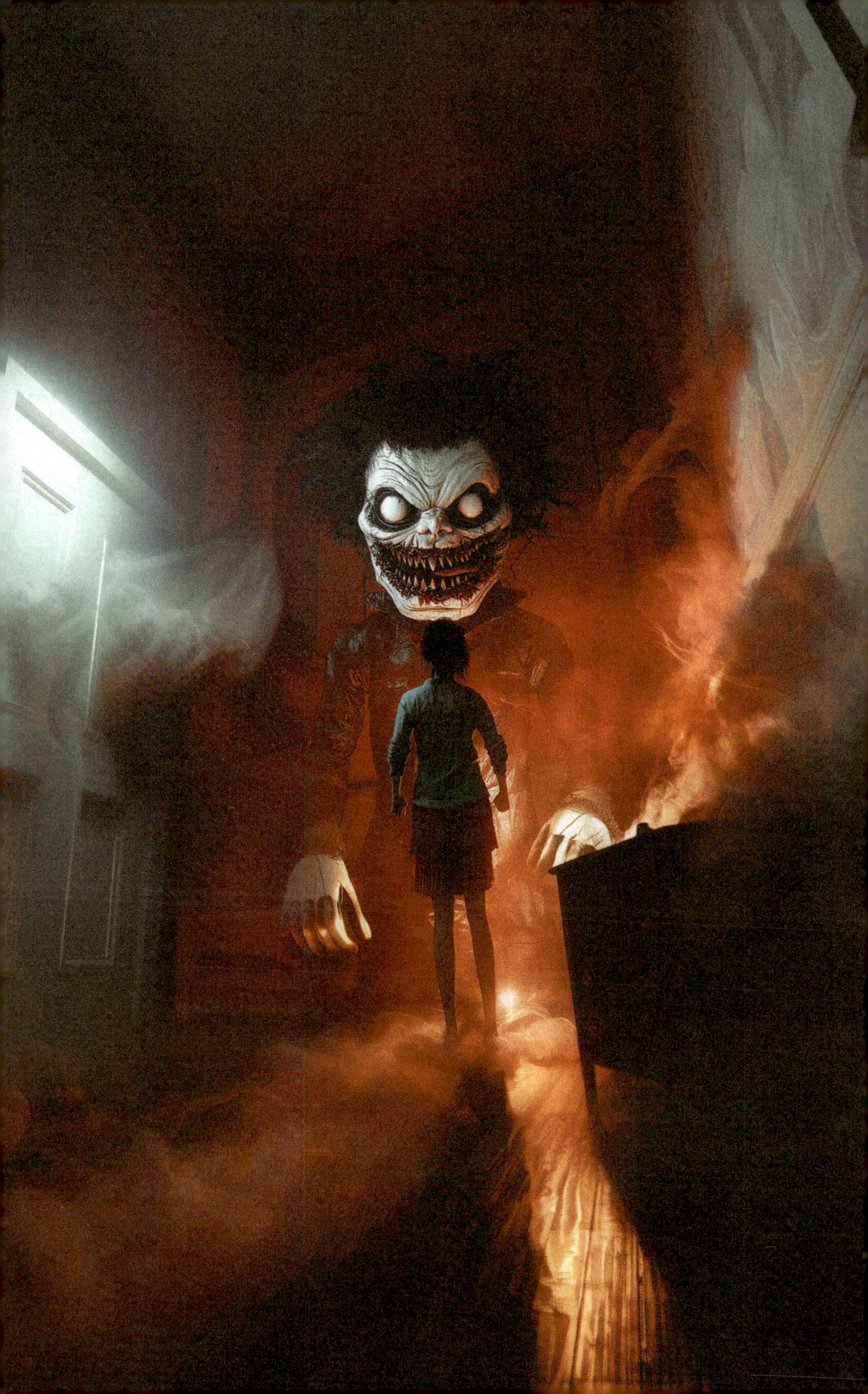

Seconds later, everything changed.

She didn't see the bobblehead's head jerk wildly or hear the frantic rattling. It was moving—alive—but Avery was already lost in sleep, unaware of the nightmare awaiting her.

She awoke in a twisted, distorted space. The walls stretched impossibly high, and the air felt suffocating. She was lying on the cold floor when she saw him.

Mister Midnight.

Now towering over her, he was a 12-foot monster with glowing eyes and an unnerving grin. The room seemed to warp around him, pulsing with unnatural energy.

"I'm bound to you now, Avery," his voice slithered in her mind, deep and resonant. "I'll leave you alone for a week if you do me a favor."

Avery's pulse quickened. "What favor?"

Without a word, he handed her a red box. The sinister grin never left his face.

"Deliver it to someone you know," he hissed. "Refuse, and you'll stay here forever."

Avery's throat went dry. She didn't dare refuse. "I'll do it," she whispered, the words tasting like ash.

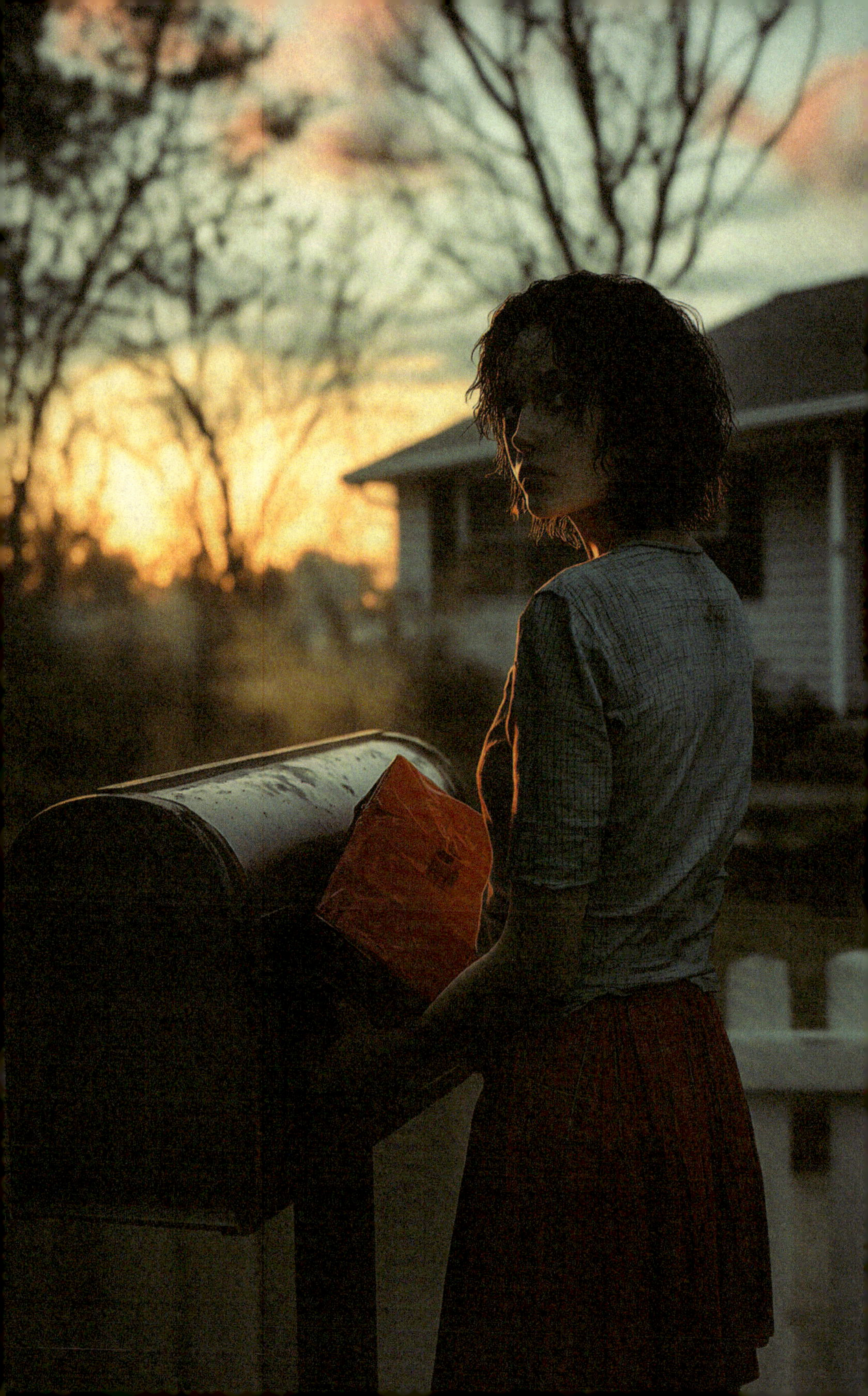

The world twisted again, and she woke in her own bed, gasping for air. Her heart thudded in her chest as her eyes locked onto the red box resting beside her. Just like in the nightmare.

Terror sank deep into her bones, but she had no choice. She grabbed the bobblehead, shoved it into a bag, and drove to the end of her street. She knew exactly who it was meant for—Mrs. Redding, her old middle school teacher, the one who had flunked her over the smallest mistake. Avery had never wanted revenge, but now—she had no choice.

At the end of the street, she dropped the red box into Mrs. Redding's mailbox. No one saw her.

A week passed. Avery lay awake most nights, the weight of Mister Midnight's looming presence keeping her restless. Tonight was the seventh night.

Then came the knock.

A red package sat on her doorstep. Avery's heart skipped. She opened it, already knowing what she would find. The bobblehead. But now, its eyes followed her every move, its grin stretching wider—far too wide. Avery's pulse raced. What would Mister Midnight demand next?

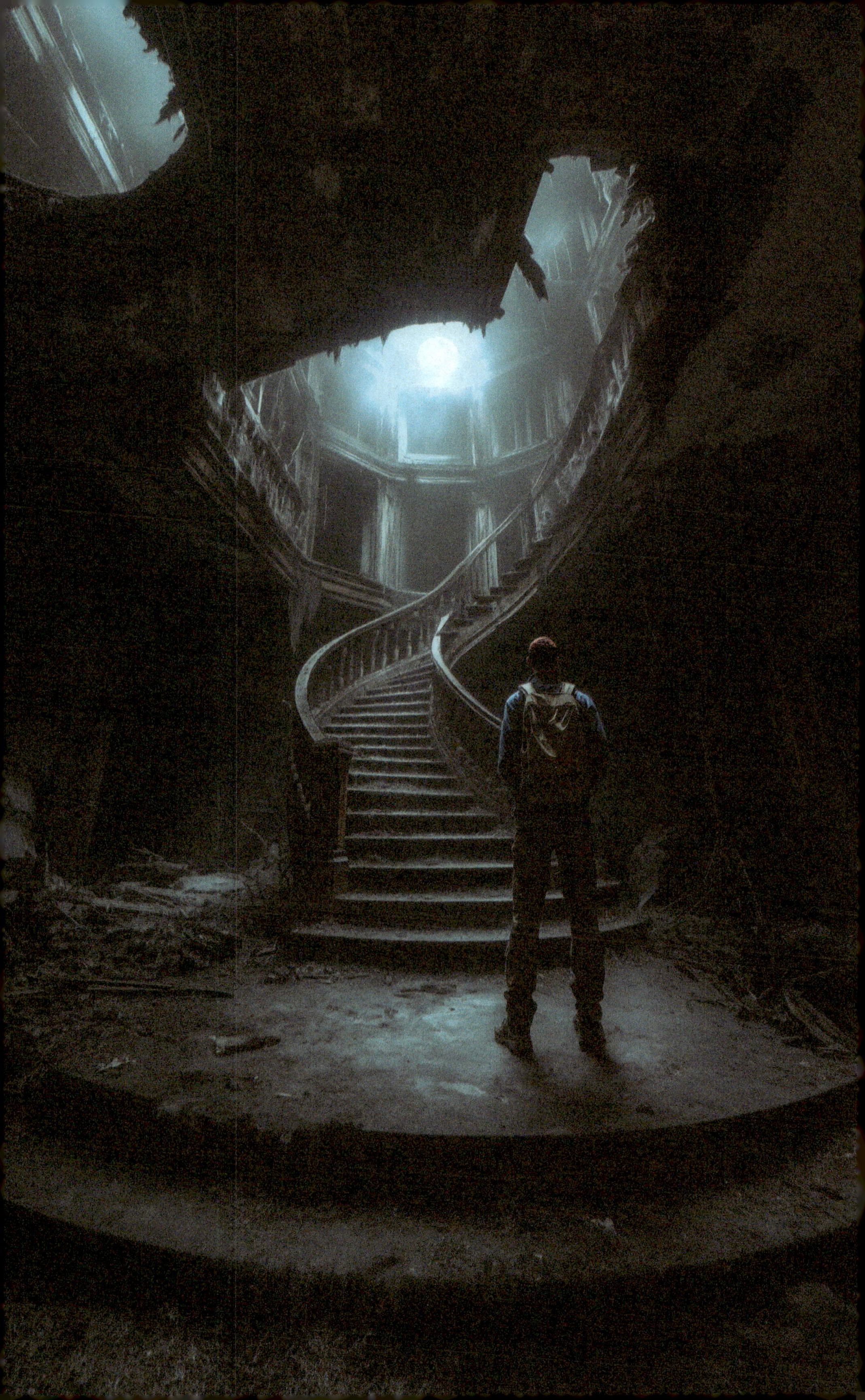

Nowhere Stairs

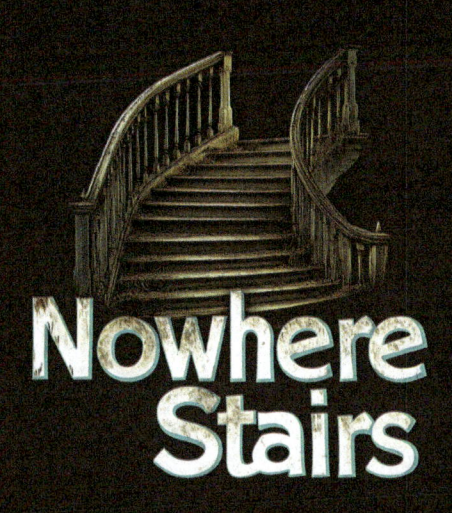

I should've never entered that house.

It's strange how time makes things smaller, how memories fade. But some parts of the past never really leave you. I didn't expect to come back to my childhood town after twenty years. Twenty years in prison, and now I was out. Fraud. I spent most of my life bending rules, until the law finally caught up.

A month after my release, I found myself driving past the old house. The house we used to call "haunted." I wasn't planning to stop. But something about it pulled me in. It didn't look the same. Smaller, rundown.

The full moon was high in the sky, casting a cold light over everything. The front door was open, hanging off its hinges. I shouldn't have gone in, but I did. The air inside was thick, stale. The place felt wrong—like something was waiting for me.

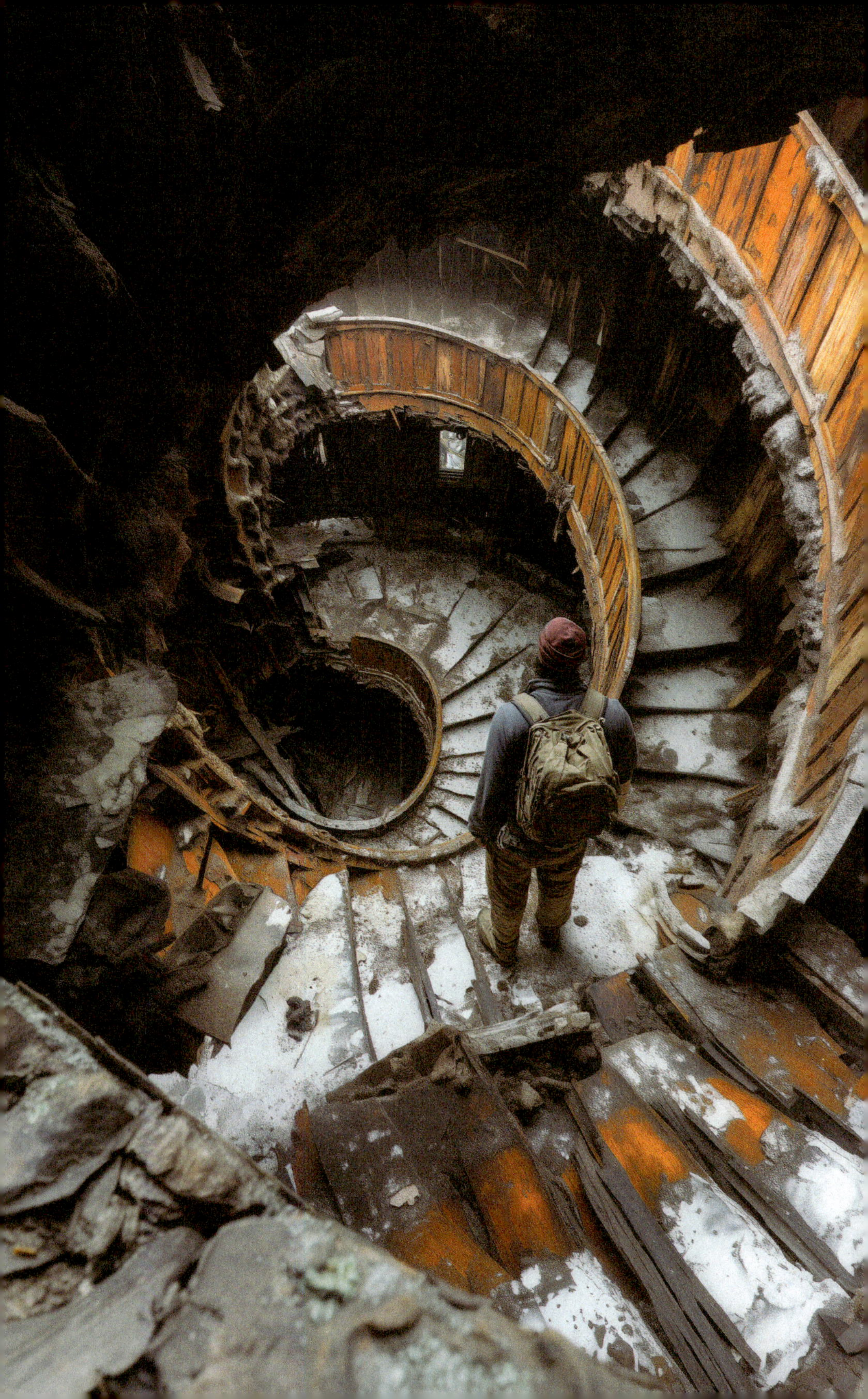

The stairs in front of me stretched up into darkness. I could feel the weight of everything pressing on me. My legs felt heavy as I climbed, a sense of vertigo creeping in. As a kid, I was always afraid of falling—falling asleep, falling from heights, falling into my own thoughts. I used to have nightmares where I was falling endlessly, waking up with my heart pounding. It never left me.

I went up anyway. The house felt endless, like it kept going higher. I passed one staircase, then another, then another. Each one more unstable than the last. It was like the house was never meant to be climbed. But I couldn't stop. I needed to see what was at the top.

Then I saw it. A spiral staircase, twisting into a darkness that didn't make sense. I turned to leave, but the way down was gone. I ran, but the house kept changing. Every turn led to more stairs, more hallways that went nowhere. It felt like I was being pulled deeper.

I tried to go down, but it didn't help. The more I went down, the darker my thoughts became. The house seemed to feed off it. The guilt. The regret. The things I'd done. It whispered to me in the dark. The people I'd hurt. The lies I'd told. I couldn't escape it.

The deeper I went, the more I realized—the house was a reflection of me. Of everything I'd tried to forget.

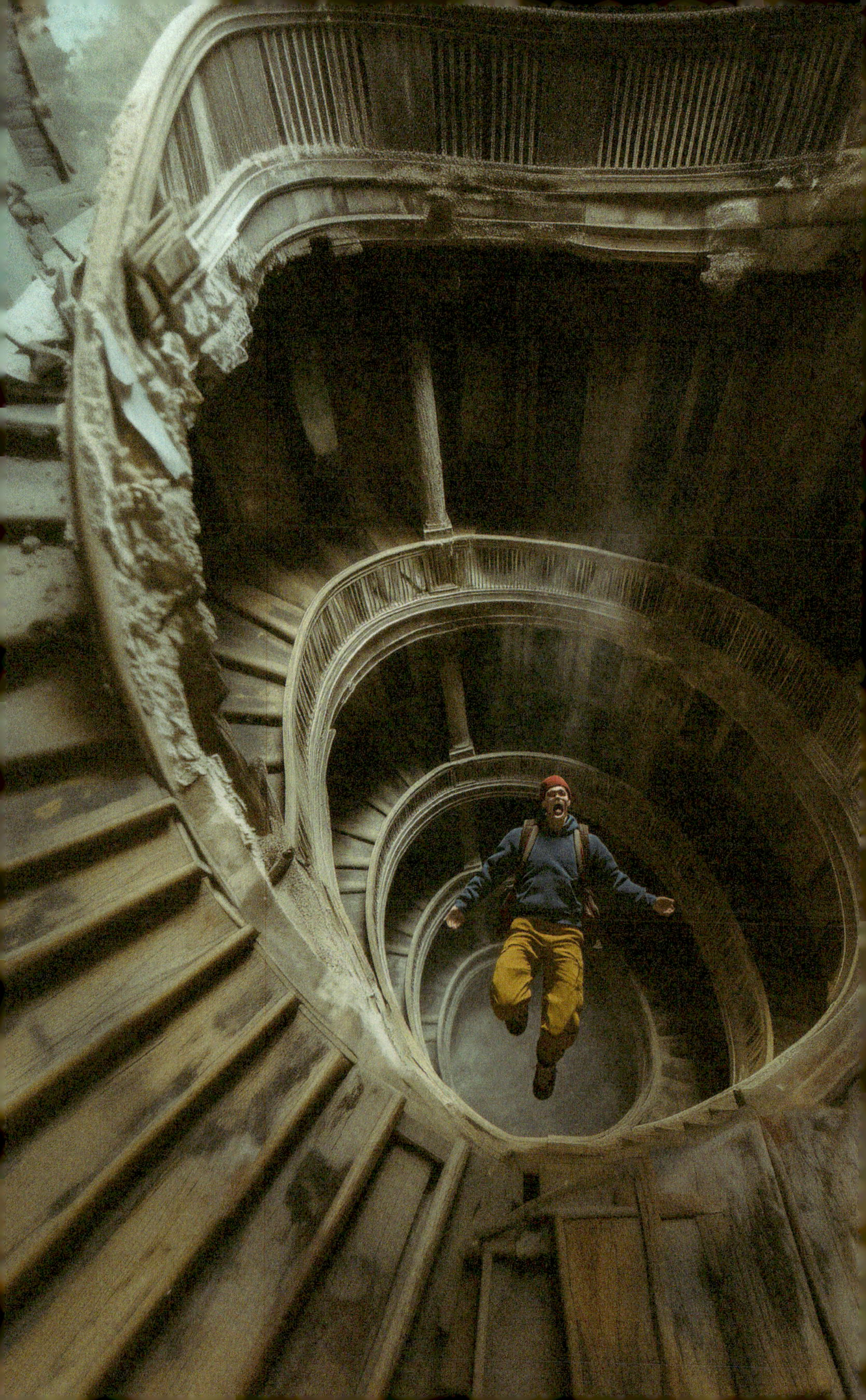

I climbed for days. Exhausted. Hopeless. Every step felt heavier. I thought if I climbed high enough, there'd be an end. But there wasn't. The house wasn't letting me go.

I stood at the edge of the staircase and looked down into the abyss below. There was no way out. No way up. No way down. Only falling.

So, I gave up.

I jumped.

I'm still falling.

And as I fall, I know the truth. The house wasn't trapping me in its walls. It was trapping me in my own mind. My own guilt. My own hell. I fell forever into the dark, and I know now—there was never an escape.

I shouldn't have entered. Now I can't leave.

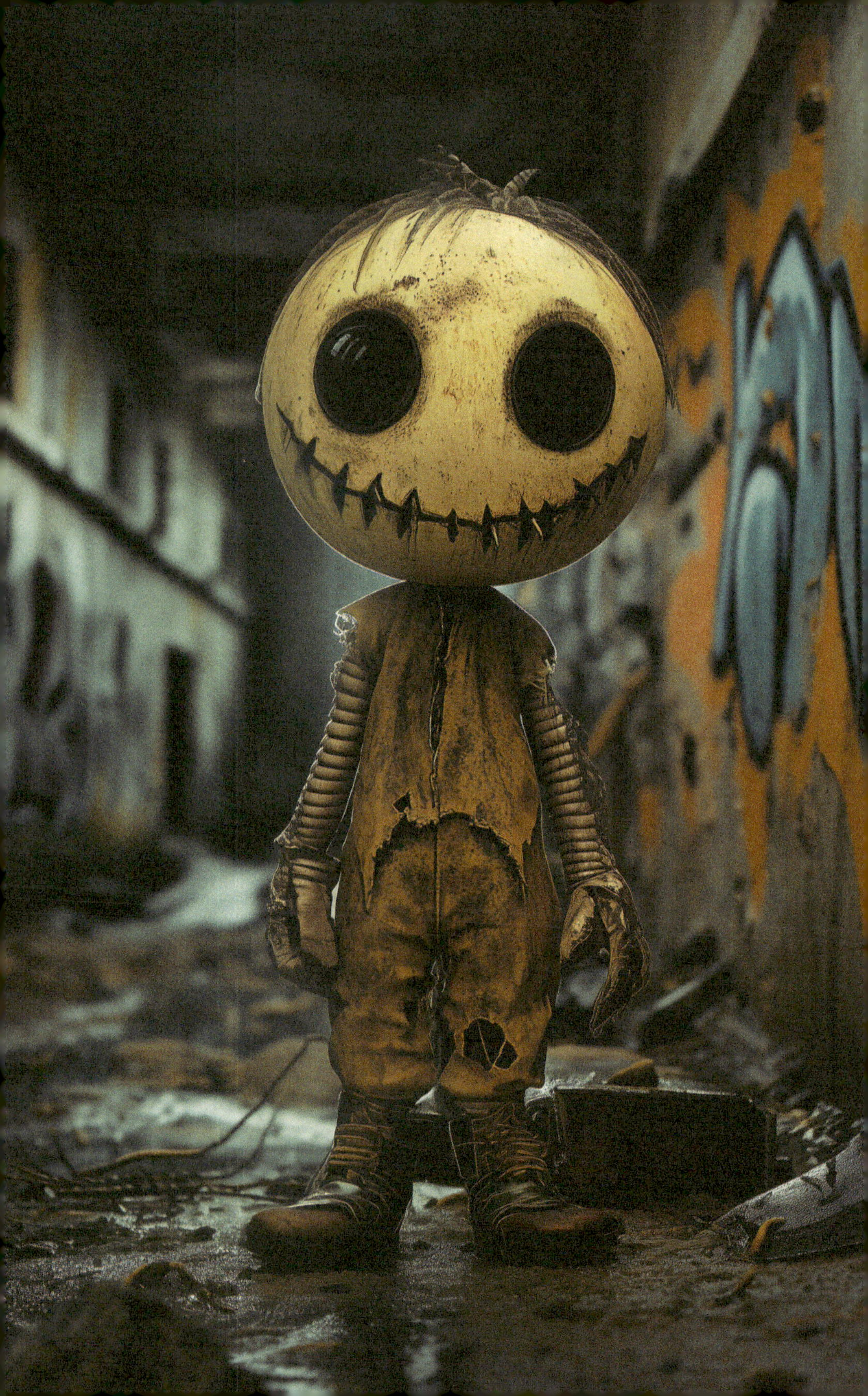

Emoji Max

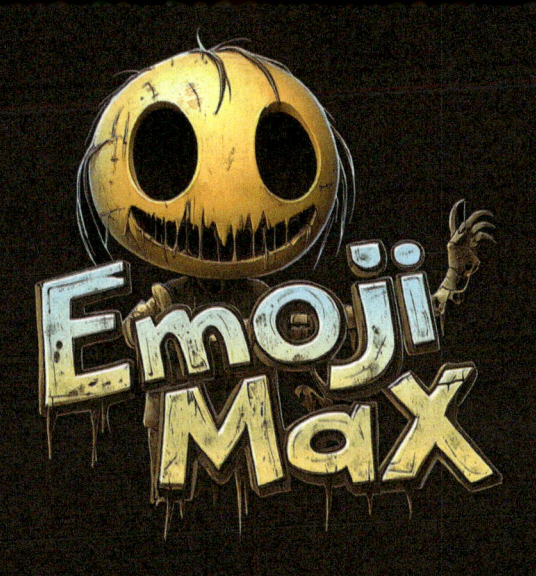

Clark had lost his job and turned to delivering food for an app called BiteBuddy. The first day went smoothly; he knew the city's streets like the back of his hand. But at 11:40 PM, instead of heading home, he accepted one last order—a decision he would regret.

The app directed him to an unfamiliar street. His headlights illuminated crumbling industrial buildings, their windows hollowed out like empty eyes.

The address led him into the parking lot of one such building. The air was damp, tinged with rust and mildew. Grabbing the delivery bag, Clark hesitated, then stepped inside.

Silence. The building yawned around him, broken beams and graffiti scrawls filling the void. He called out, but only his echo responded. Just as he turned to leave, a figure emerged from behind a cracked pillar, moving in an awkward, sideways shuffle.

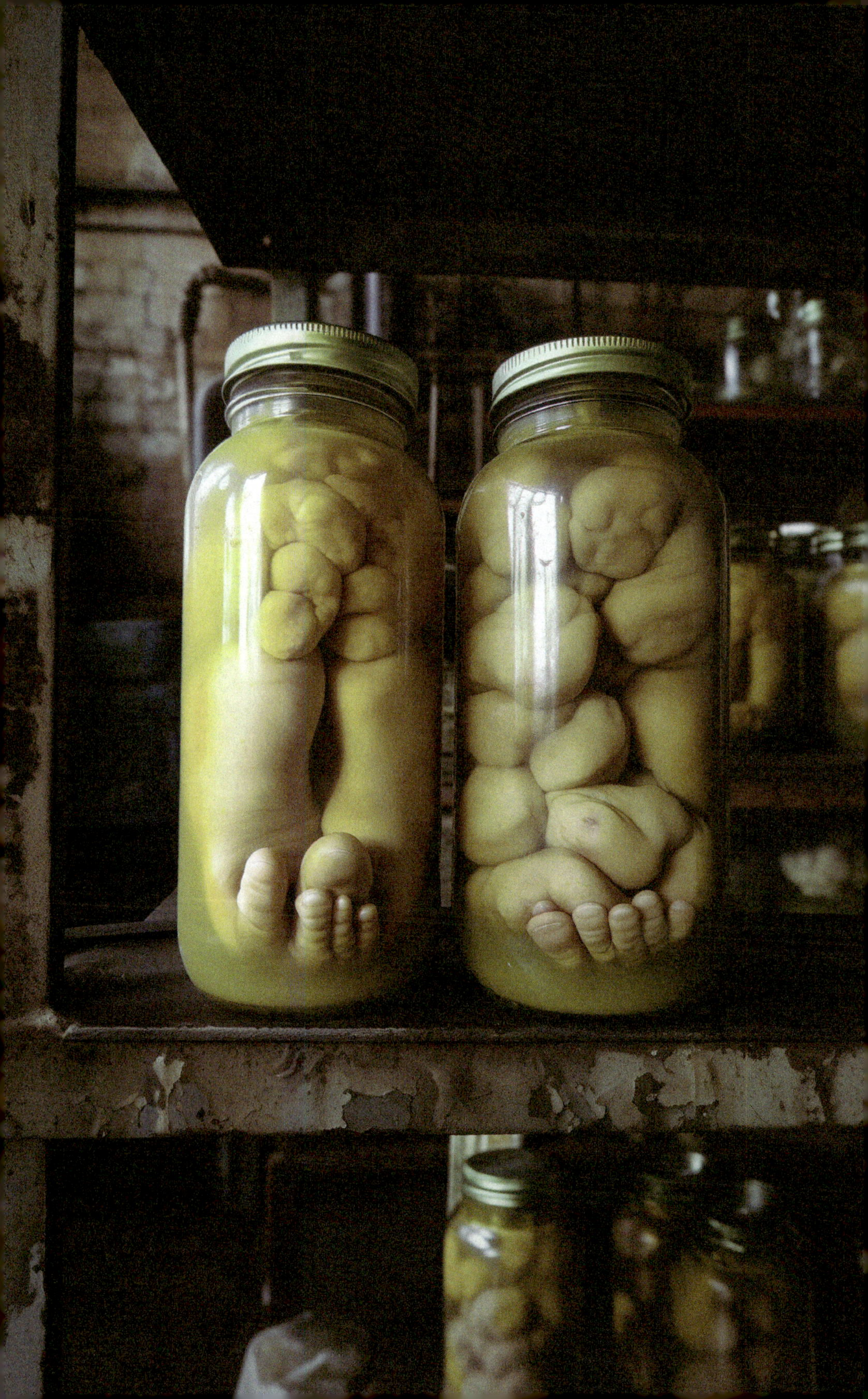

It was Emoji Max.

Five feet tall, metal body draped in tattered brown rags. A giant yellow head, like a warped emoji, grinned at Clark with jagged teeth, large black eyes hollow and staring.

"I'm here for the delivery," Clark blurted, unsure what else to say.
"Follow me," Emoji Max replied, his voice a grating monotone. "The Won Ton soup is in the other room."

Max shuffled sideways through a doorway, and despite every instinct telling him to run, Clark followed. The adjacent room was dimly lit by a flickering, overhead bulb.

Glass jars lined the shelves, their contents swimming in a murky liquid—twisted flesh, hair tufts, and a toe or two pressing against the glass. The air was thick, rancid.

Clark gagged. "What... what's in these?"
"You don't want to know," Max replied, handing Clark a bill—over $500. The delivery address glowed on Clark's phone.

The potential tip clouded his better judgment. He punched the address into the app, convinced he'd score big. "Will you need more deliveries?" he asked, voice shaking.

Max's jagged grin widened. "We'll be in touch."

Clark left, his tires screeching through the desolate lot. He drove across town, eyes darting to the rearview mirror. Mid-

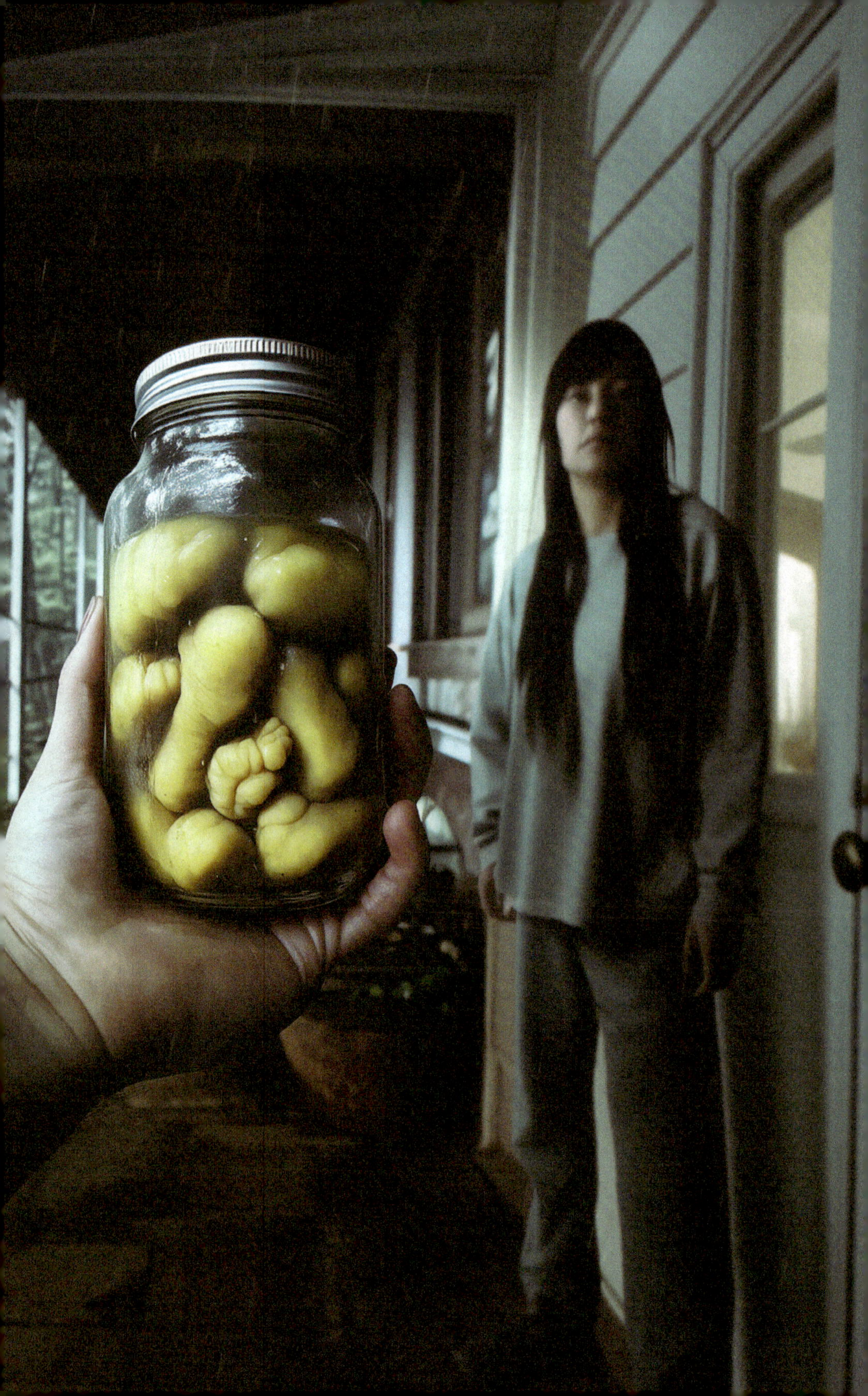

night struck as he pulled into a neat suburban driveway. The porch light flicked on, and a woman with hollow eyes stepped forward. She took the jar without a word.

Clark handed her his card. "Call me directly," he said, his voice strained but eager. "If you need more."

She smiled—thin and joyless. He drove home, clutching his phone, waiting for the next notification. Waiting for someone else who needed what was in those jars. Waiting for Emoji Max.

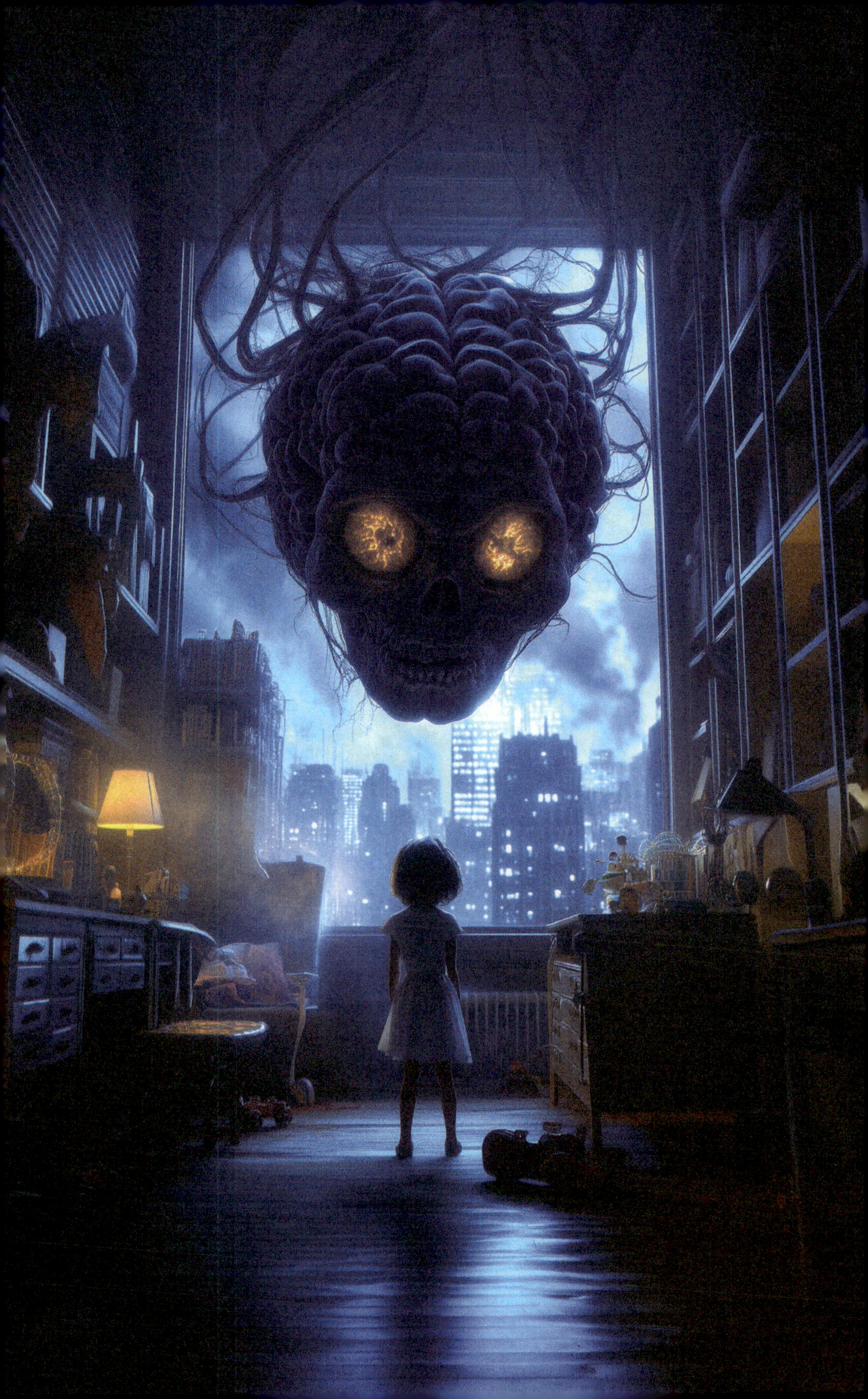

Brainstorm Lullaby

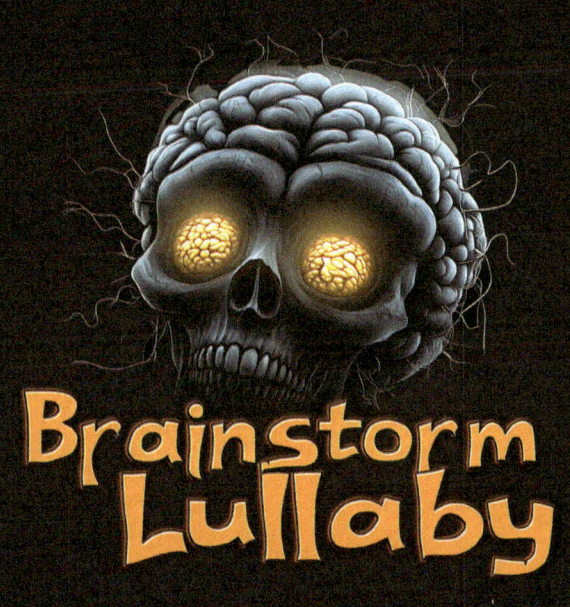

Destiny wasn't a normal child. At 5 years old, she was already known for her strange stories, especially about the "brain creature" that visited her at night. Her parents didn't believe her. They thought it was just a mix of imagination and nightmares. But they'd had enough. When Halloween came around, Destiny was grounded. It was supposed to be her first time trick-or-treating, but instead, she was locked in her room of their high-rise loft, alone.

From her window, Destiny could see the children below, laughing and running through the streets, collecting candy. It was dark already, 6 PM, when the creature appeared. She called him Mr. Squishy. He wasn't like anything anyone could imagine—half brain, half face, with pulsing veins wrapped around him like tentacles, and glowing yellow eyes that locked onto hers whenever he showed up. Her heart raced. Destiny's smile spread across her face as she dropped her princess crown and ran to the window. "Hi, Mr.

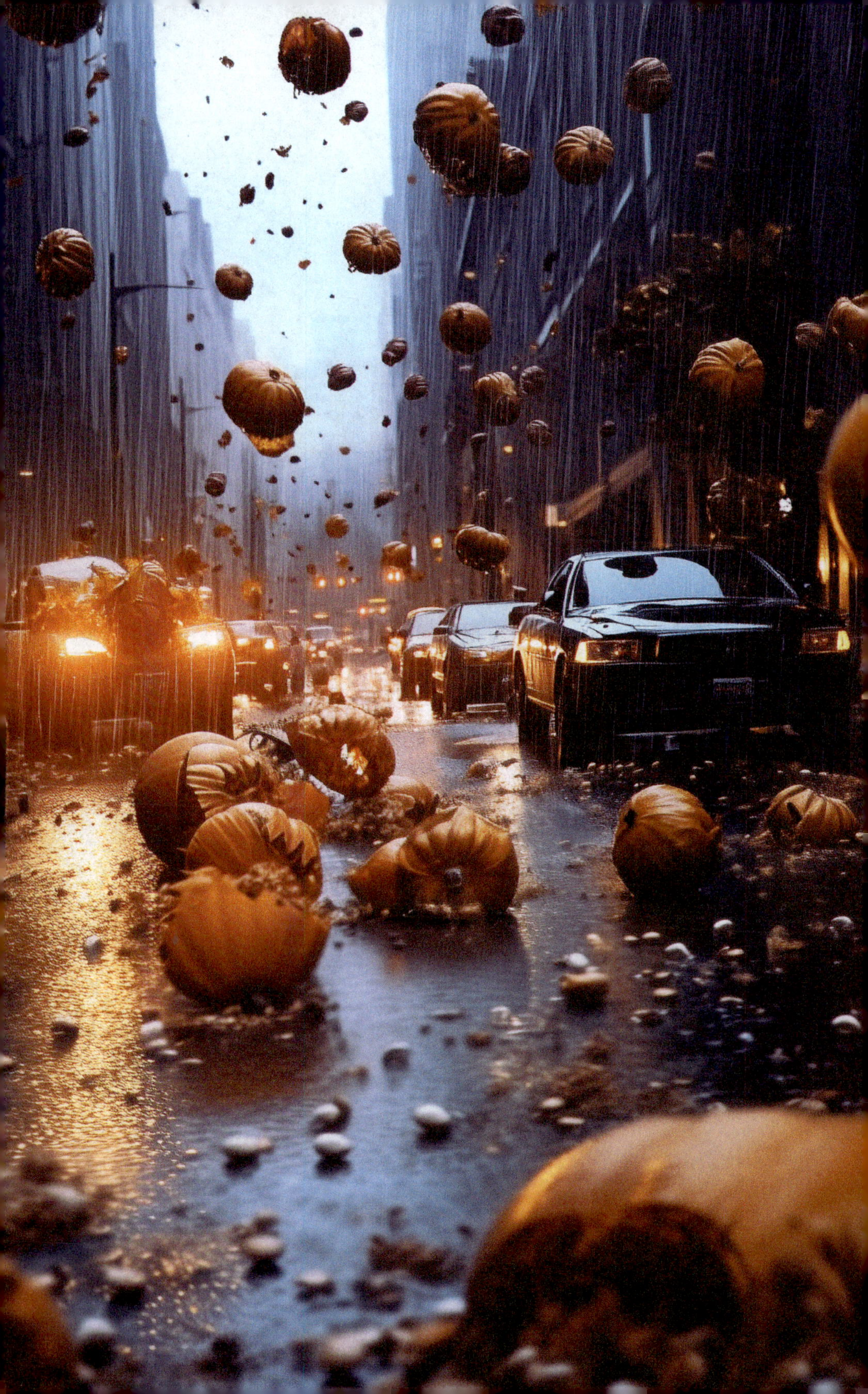

Squishy," she whispered. "I can't go trick-or-treating. Did you bring me candy?"

Mr. Squishy didn't speak, but candy began to spill from his glowing eyes. The air filled with the thick, sticky sweetness of sugar, and Destiny's hands shook as she gathered it into her pumpkin-shaped bucket. It was a routine now: whatever she wished for would come true if she touched him.

She had learned this the hard way the last two times they'd met. The first time, Destiny wished for all her toys to come to life, and they had started moving on their own, scaring her parents. The second time, she wished for her room to be filled with candy, and it had spilled out of her closet until the whole floor was covered. Her parents had no answers and only scolded her, but no one could stop Mr. Squishy.

Her fingers brushed his cold face, and a dark thought crossed her mind. If I can't have Halloween, then no one will.

She closed her eyes, and the thought formed. A pumpkin storm. Pumpkins falling from the sky.

When she opened her eyes, she saw it. Pumpkins, massive and heavy, were crashing down from the heavens. The first one hit the ground with a deafening crack, shattering and splintering into pieces. The rest followed, each one smashing into the buildings and cars below. The streets turned orange as pumpkins flooded the ground. Destiny giggled, pressing her face to the window, delighting in the chaos below.

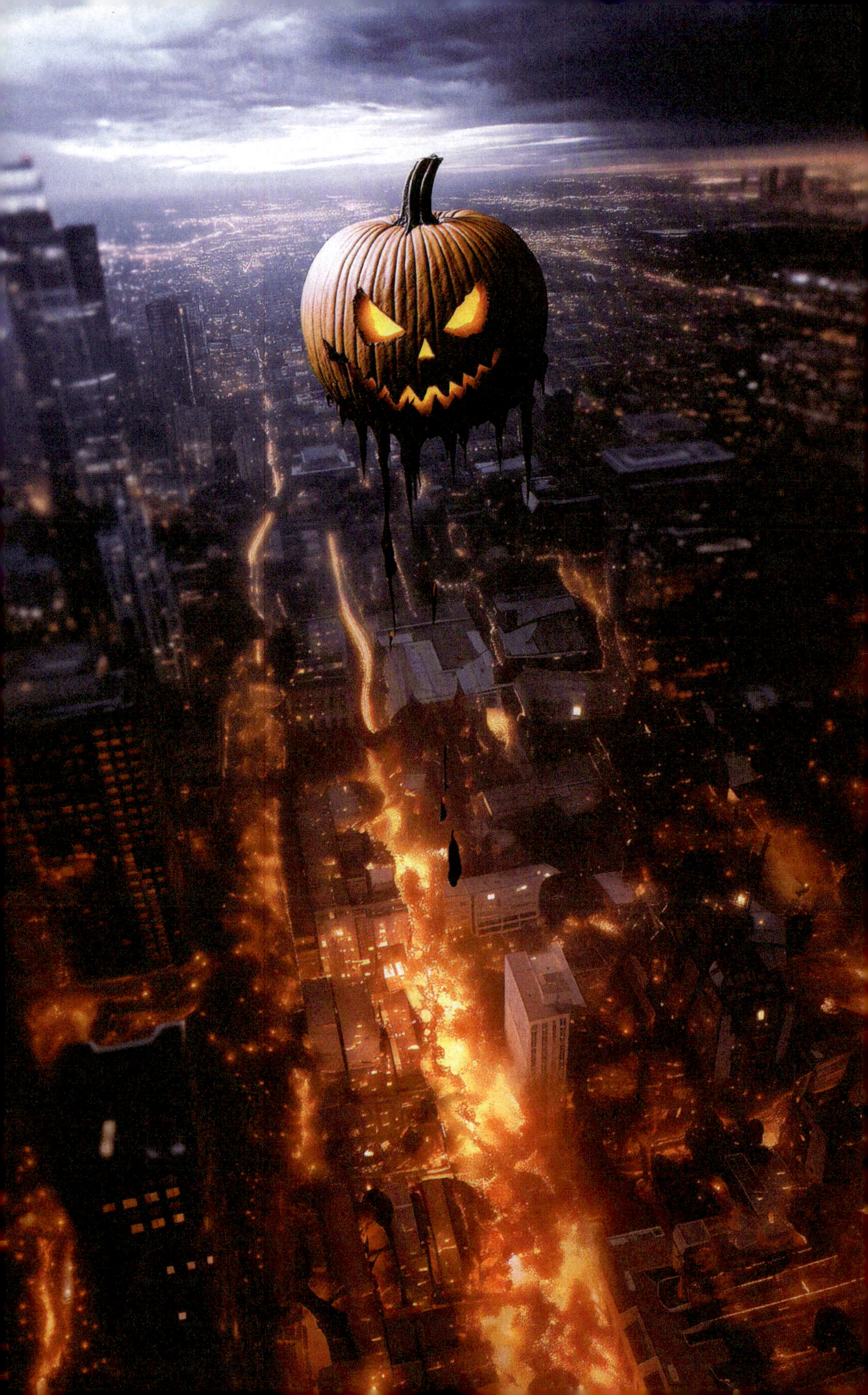

But that wasn't enough. She wanted more. She imagined a pumpkin so big, so monstrous, that it would swallow everything. It grew, bigger and bigger, until it hovered over the city, dropping endless candy. The ground shook as it descended, and the candy fell like bombs, hitting the streets and buildings, destroying everything in its path. Destiny's heart raced as she watched the destruction unfold.

The destruction didn't stop there. Her mind twisted with darker thoughts. What else could she wish for? She imagined the pumpkins coming to life, their jagged mouths opening wide, eyes burning with fire. They would burn the city. Tear it apart. Then, the candy would turn to flames, spreading across the streets, igniting everything it touched. The sky itself would crack open, raining fire and terror. The pumpkins came alive, stomping through the streets, their fiery eyes glowing as they hunted down everything in their path. The city was consumed by flames as the pumpkins destroyed everything in sight. Destiny laughed, clapping her hands as the fire spread. Her twisted Halloween wish had come true.

The city was gone. Burned to the ground by her desires.

Destiny stood at the window, her face pressed against the cold glass, eyes wide with glee. I took Halloween from them all, she thought. But as the fires raged, another thought crept into her mind. What else could she wish for? More destruction. More chaos.

Mr. Squishy floated nearby, waiting, as if he knew the answer. And Destiny... she wasn't done yet.

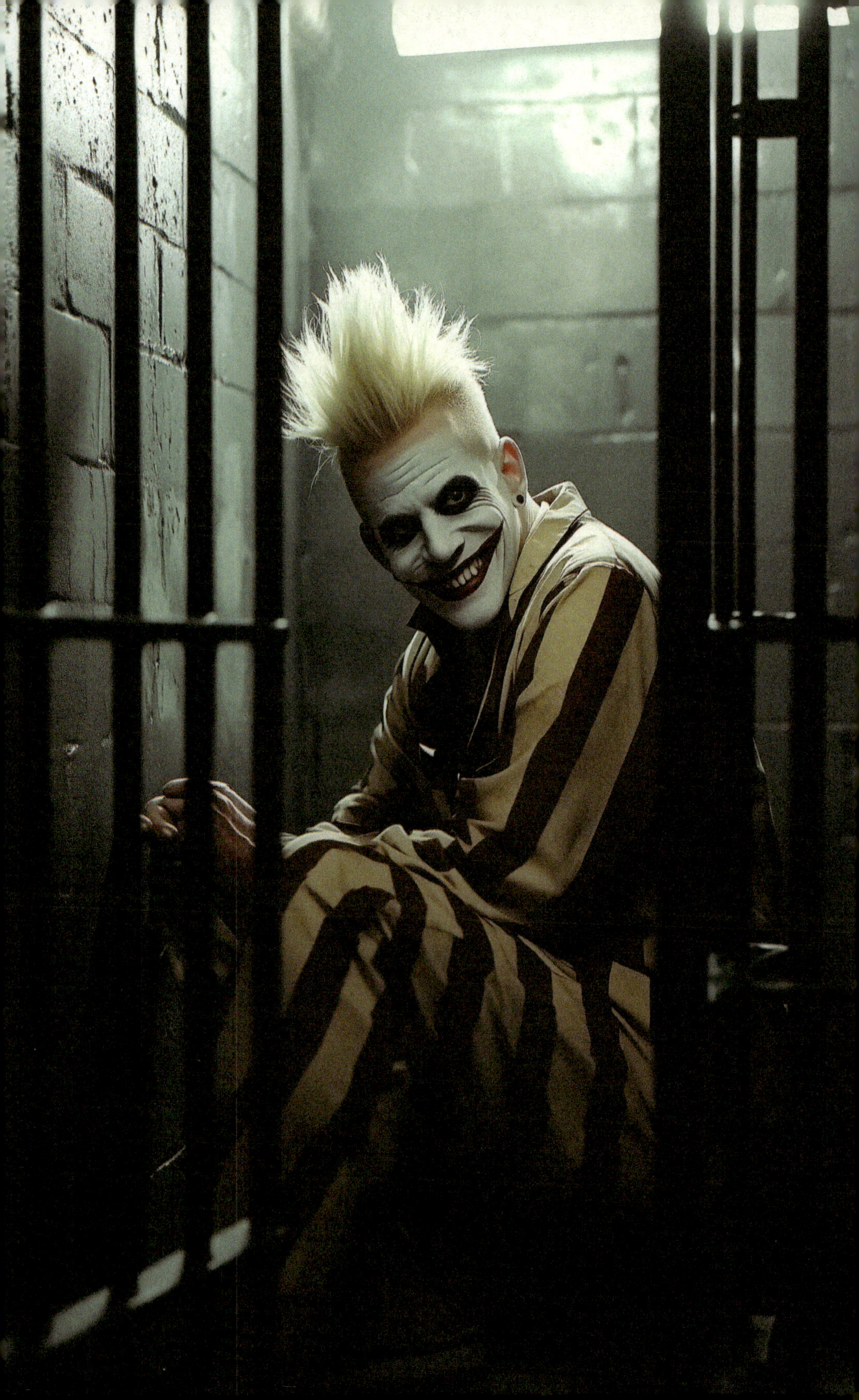

Grim Exit

Cameron had been committed to the state penitentiary for second-degree murder. The first day he walked to his cell, he noticed inmates with faces painted white—hollow eyes, smeared lipstick, and strange symbols etched in shadowy greasepaint.

It didn't take long for Cameron to learn they were members of a cult. They worshipped something in the prison walls, a spirit that demanded to be fed. Stories spread like wildfire: guards gone missing, inmates vanishing without a trace. The creature, they whispered, only hunted those foolish enough to wander the hidden tunnels and forgotten wings of the prison.

Days passed before Cameron encountered Lazarus. Tall, with spiked blond hair, a face painted ghostly white, and a grin as wild as it was menacing, Lazarus was unlike the others. "Hey, new blood," he whispered one night, motioning for Cameron to come closer.

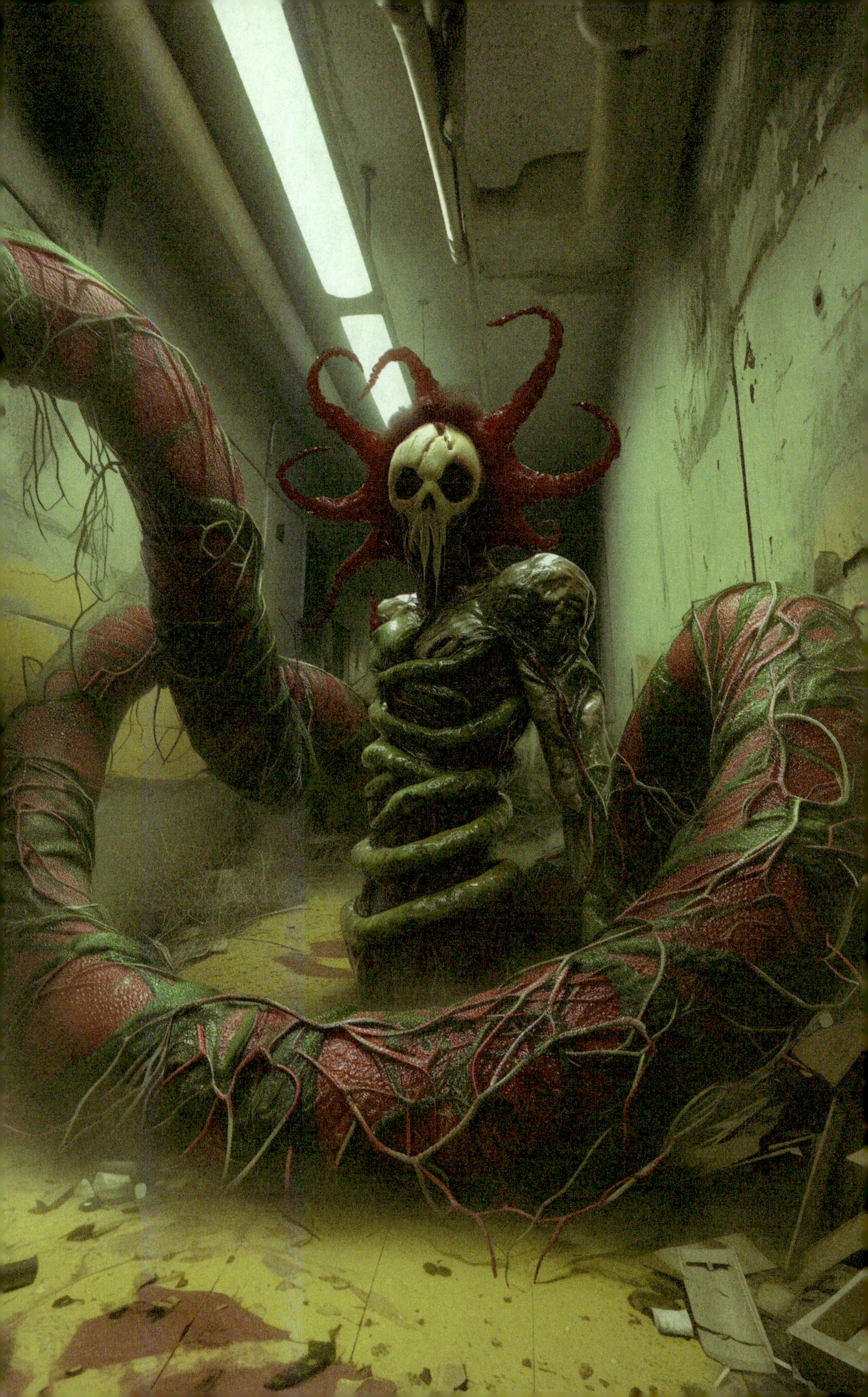

Against his better judgment, Cameron approached. Lazarus's eyes gleamed. "For a hundred bucks, I'll tell you how to get out," he said, his voice a low rasp. He leaned in, the scent of rot clinging to him. "There's a tunnel, through the abandoned wing. Leads outside. No bars, no guards."

Cameron asked the obvious question: "Then why haven't you escaped?"

Lazarus chuckled, a sound like breaking glass. "Because of it." His voice turned cold. "The thing in the walls. Like a snake, but worse. It has a human skull for a face. It'll either catch you or... maybe you're lucky and it doesn't. You can run, or stay silent. But don't get caught."

That night, Cameron prepared. He traded for makeshift weapons—sharpened shanks, a crude club—and finally, he found the cabinet Lazarus had described, pushing it aside to reveal a gaping hole in the wall.

The air beyond was damp and reeked of rot. He squeezed through, flashlight in hand, and found himself in a corridor that stretched into darkness. The walls were crumbling, the floor slick, and the ceiling hung low enough to make him crouch.

He walked, stepping over debris and broken furniture, every sound echoing like a gunshot in the dead silence. The further he went, the worse the smell became—decay, old blood, and something worse: anticipation. He passed doorways

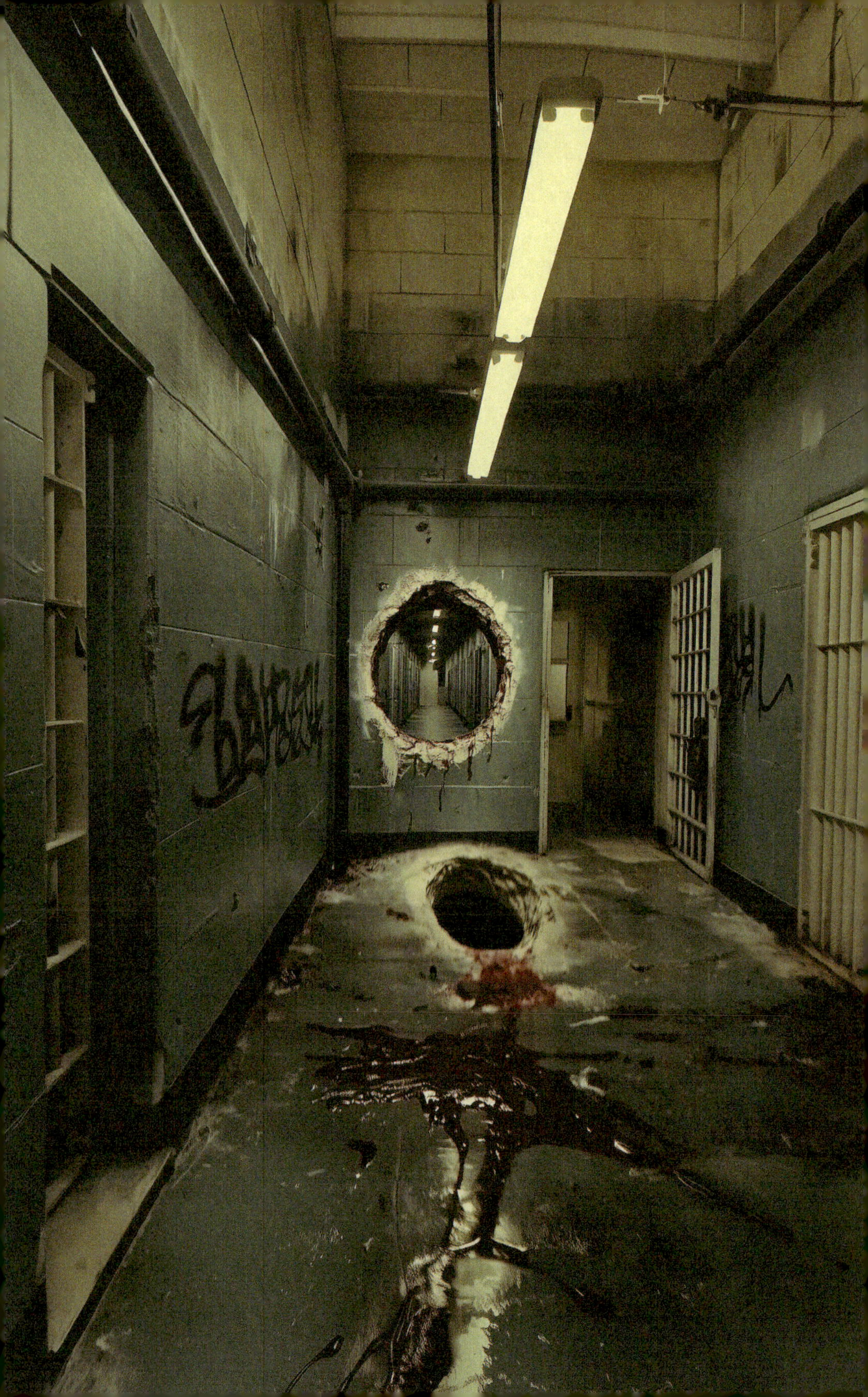

leading into empty, forgotten rooms. He could feel eyes on him. No, not eyes—something else.

Then he heard it. A scraping, slithering sound from behind him. His blood ran cold. Cameron turned, heart pounding, and saw it. It was exactly as Lazarus had said: a snake-like thing, massive and glistening, with scales of red and green.

But its face—its face was a bleached, grinning human skull, empty sockets fixed on him. It tilted its head, the bones cracking, and hissed, "Run."

Cameron didn't move. He couldn't. The thing surged forward, a blur of muscle and bone, and before he could even lift his shank, it was on him. It dragged him, screaming, down the tunnels, faster than he could comprehend, past twisting passages and into a chamber lined with skulls.

The last thing Cameron saw was the darkness closing in, the snake-man's skeletal grin, and the sharp, horrible truth: he wasn't meant to escape.

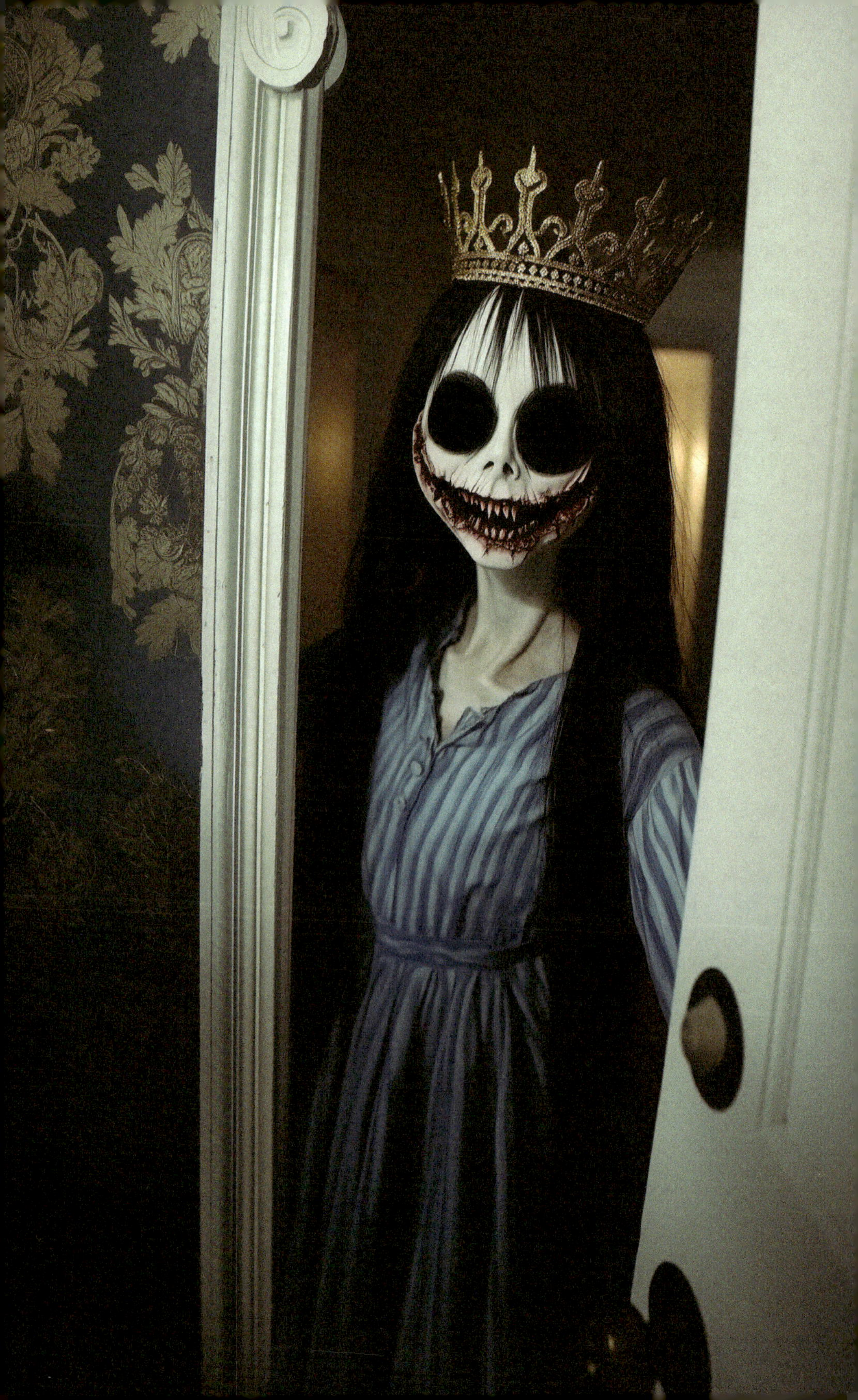

Screaming Lily

Adam's controlling and demanding girlfriend had taken her own life after he cheated on her.

Devastated, he scoured her social media from her phone, learning things about her life that left him feeling conflicted with both sadness and resentment.

Despite his suspicions, he couldn't find any proof of his own infidelity, but there were signs of her paranoia — jealous rants and obsessive investigations into his life.

How much had she known about his secret?

On the seventh night after her death, it happened.

He had fallen asleep on the couch, drifting off during a game show, only to be jolted awake by an otherworldly scream.

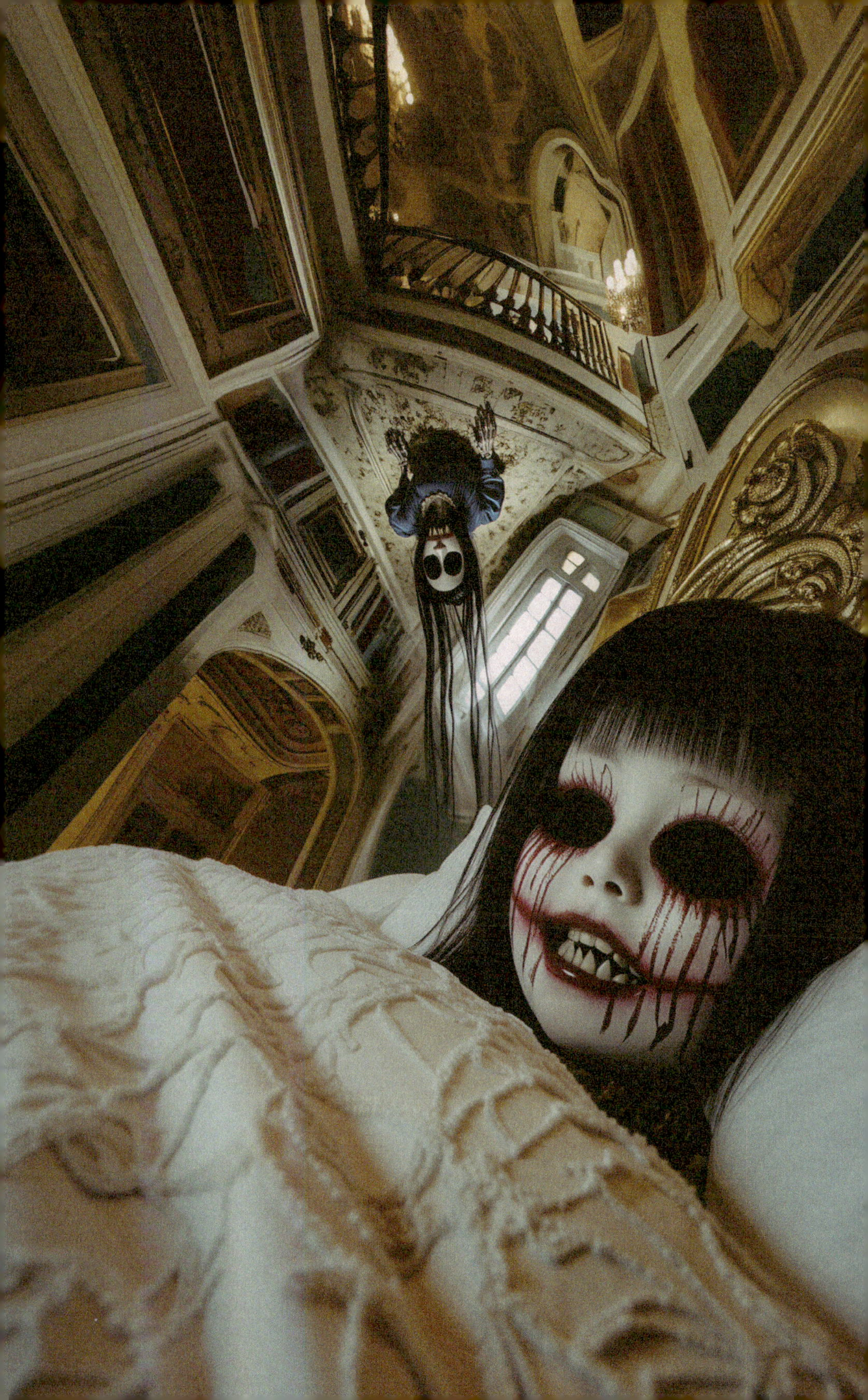

He found himself staring at the doorway, where she stood — her ghost, grinning unnaturally with hollow black eyes, as if to warn him that she would return. The smile stretched wider, impossibly so, and her eyes seemed to burn through him, as if she could see every dark corner of his soul. He tried to look away, but the force of her presence pinned him in place, her chilling laughter echoing in his mind long after she disappeared.

The haunting repeated every time Adam fell asleep.

Her ghost would torment him, pushing him further into sleepless madness.

No matter where he tried to hide—friends' homes, hotels, even a cardboard box—she found him, her presence unshakable.

She wasn't haunting his house; she was haunting him.

One night, desperate for peace, Adam armed himself with a shovel, determined to confront her ghost.

He swung at her, disfiguring her spectral form.

But when he fell asleep once again, exhausted beyond belief, she screamed in his ear, more terrifying than before.

The damage he had done had made her even more grotesque, more menacing.

And so it continued. Adam couldn't escape.

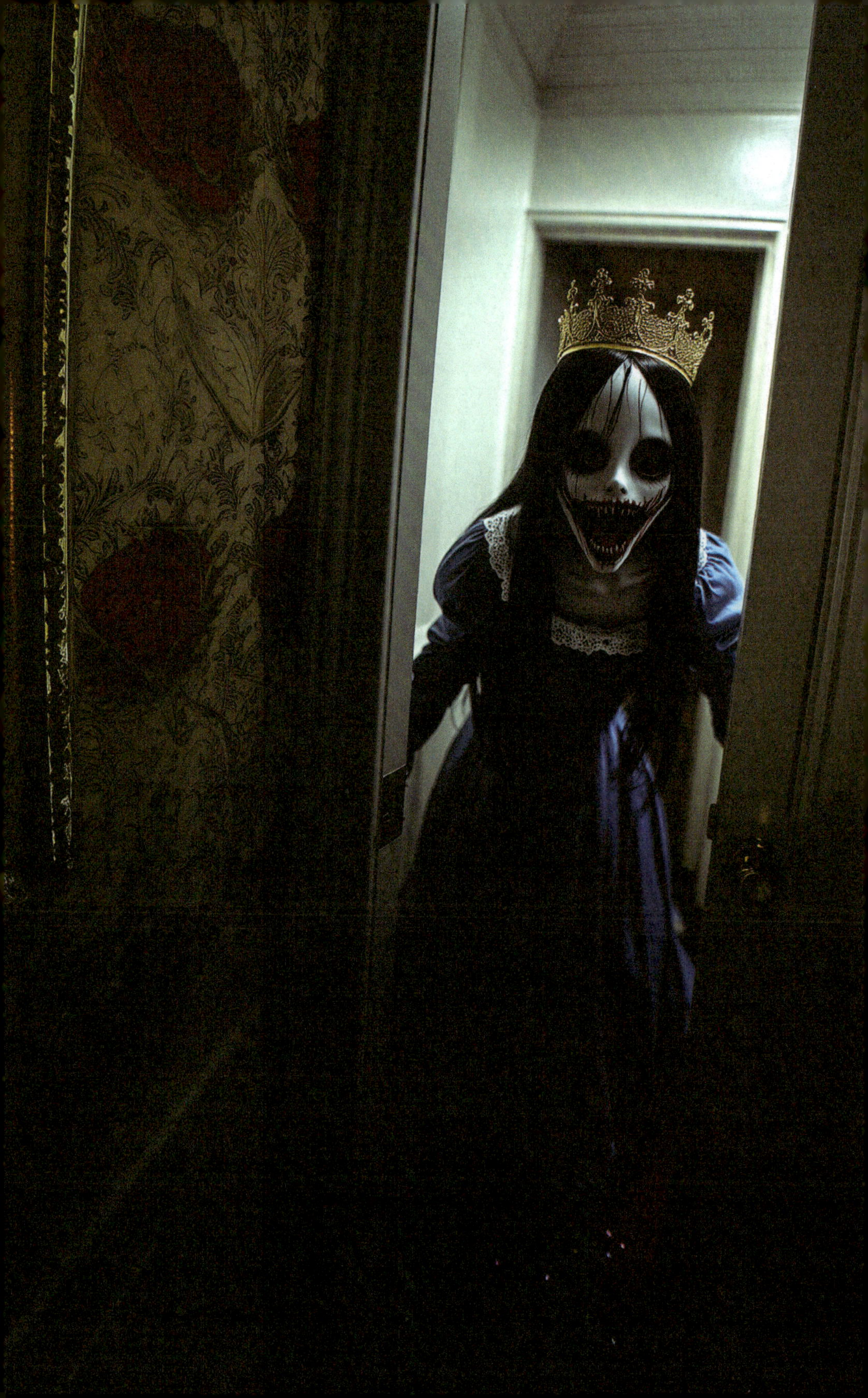

The ghost of his dead girlfriend was always with him, twisted and worse with each passing night.

Eventually, Adam's mind broke under the weight of the torment.

He was institutionalized, diagnosed with severe insomnia and schizophrenia.

There, he spent the rest of his life, never free from the chilling presence of his deceased lover.

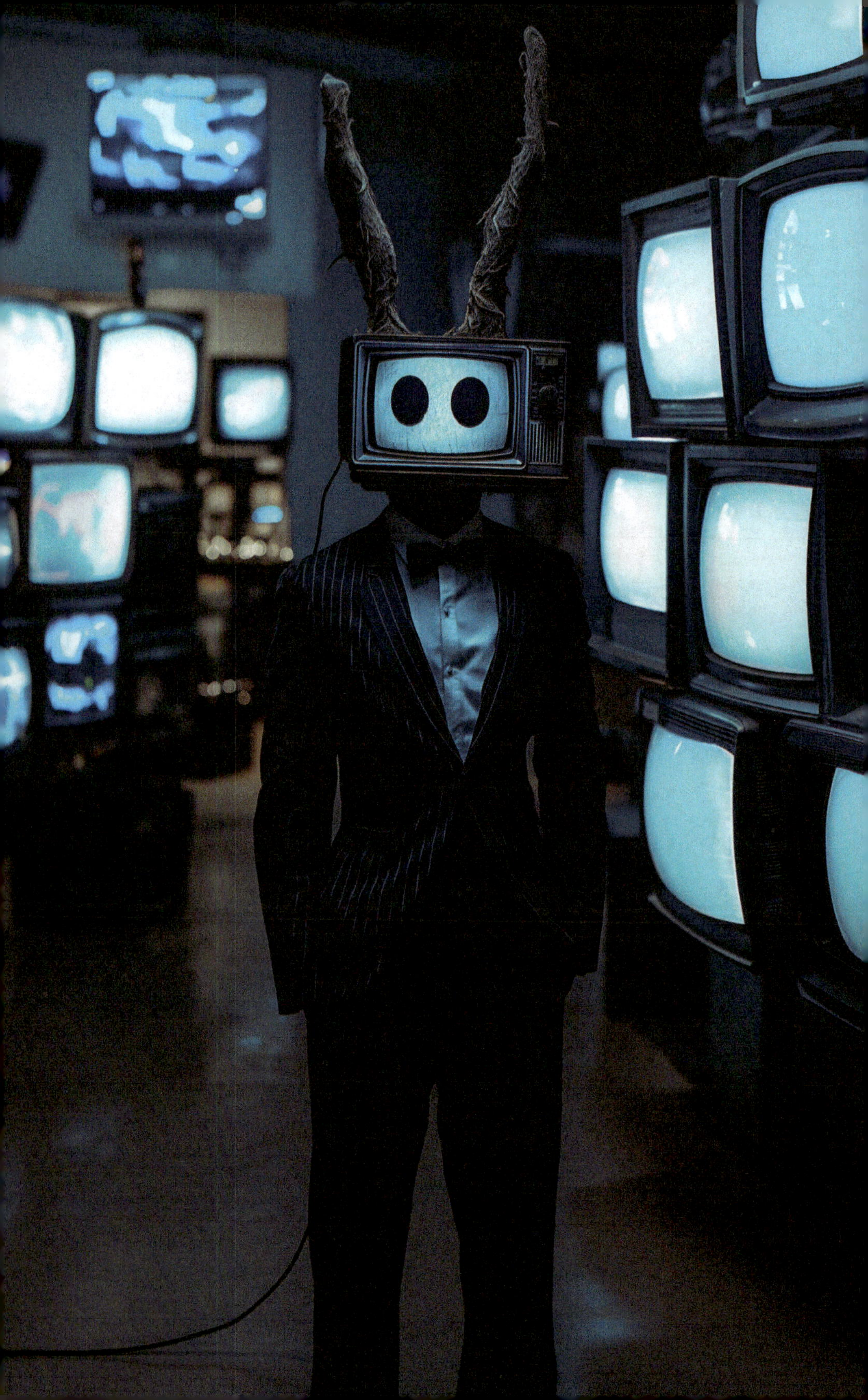

Static Black

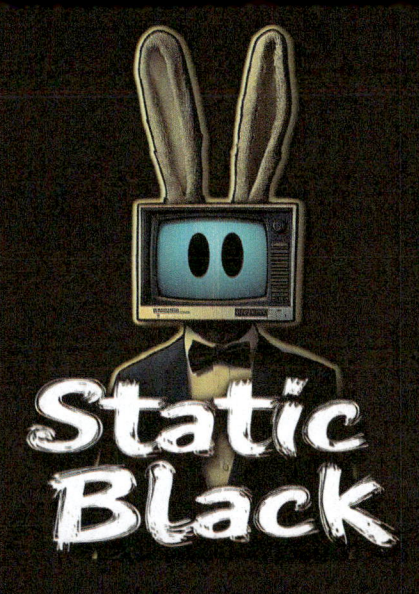

Liam and Noah had been best friends since childhood, chasing every strange thrill they could find. So when Static Black, the creepy TV store, announced its one-hour reopening, they had to see it. They'd grown up watching its weird late-night commercials. Dim lighting, rows of old cathode-ray TVs glowing with static, and him.

Static Black.

A man—or something—in a sleek black suit, his head a small TV buzzing with white noise. In the static, two black eyes floated, empty but watching. Worst of all were the rabbit ears—twitching like broken antennas. Was he animatronic? A man in a suit? No one knew.

"Think we'll meet him?" Liam grinned as they stumbled out of the car, drunk.

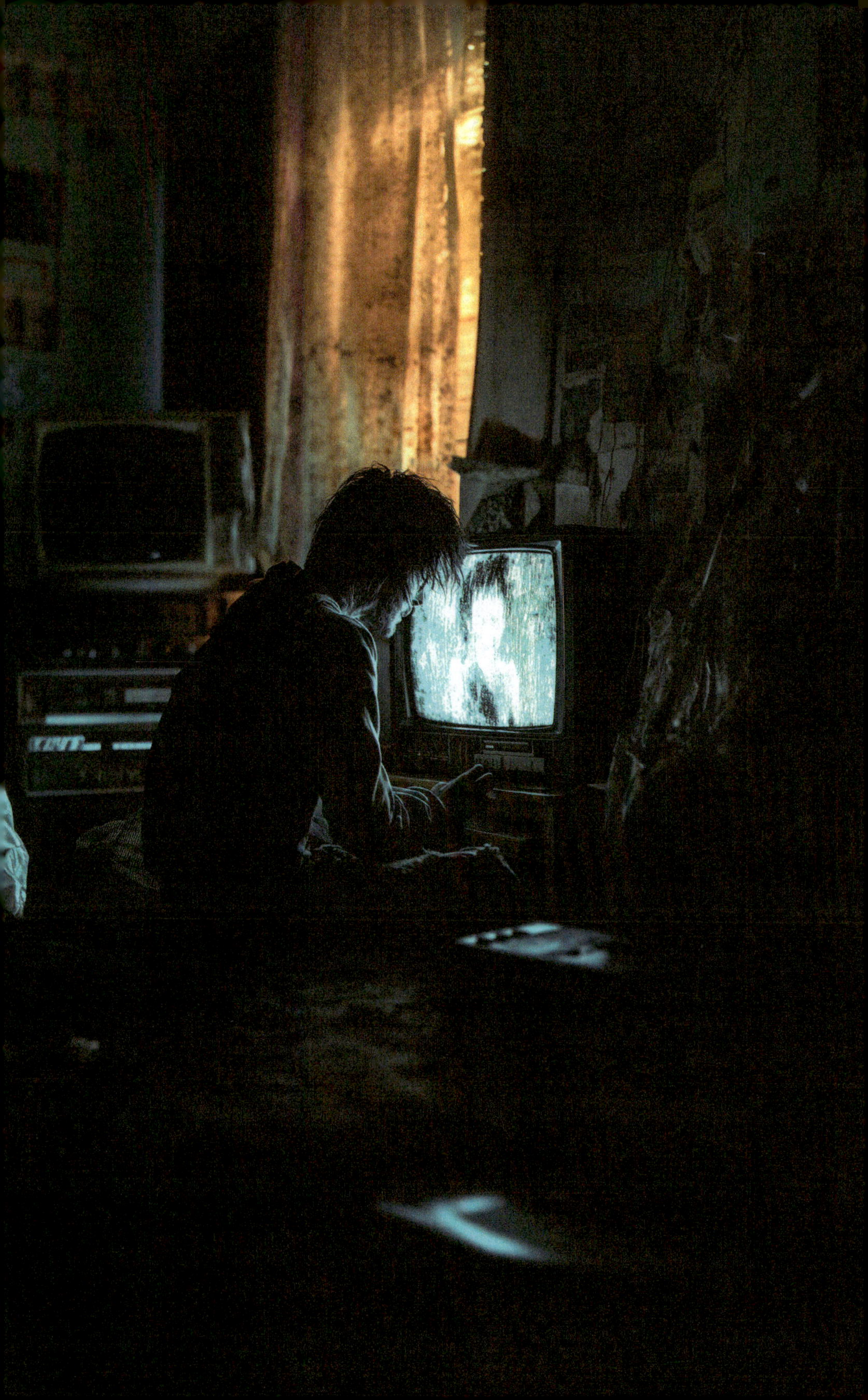

"He better give you a birthday discount," Noah joked, pushing the door open.

Inside, the air smelled like dust and electricity. Blue static from rows of TVs bathed the room in an eerie glow. Then, from the shadows, he appeared.

Static Black.

He stood perfectly still, static crackling from his TV head. "Welcome," he said, his voice distorted and distant. "Find the television meant for you. The static speaks."

"How do we know which one's ours?" Noah asked nervously.

"The static will tell you," Static Black replied. "It binds to you... if you listen."

They left with two TVs. Liam remembered choosing his. Noah didn't. He didn't even want it. But later that night, he couldn't resist. He plugged it in. Turned the dial. Static. He stared into the noise until sleep overtook him.

Each night, the static whispered. It told him things—secrets he couldn't understand but couldn't ignore. Then, one night, it stopped. And Noah woke up afraid.

Then he disappeared. No warning, no goodbye. Just gone.

A year later, Liam sat alone. One night, after watching a tape, the static returned. Louder. Angry.

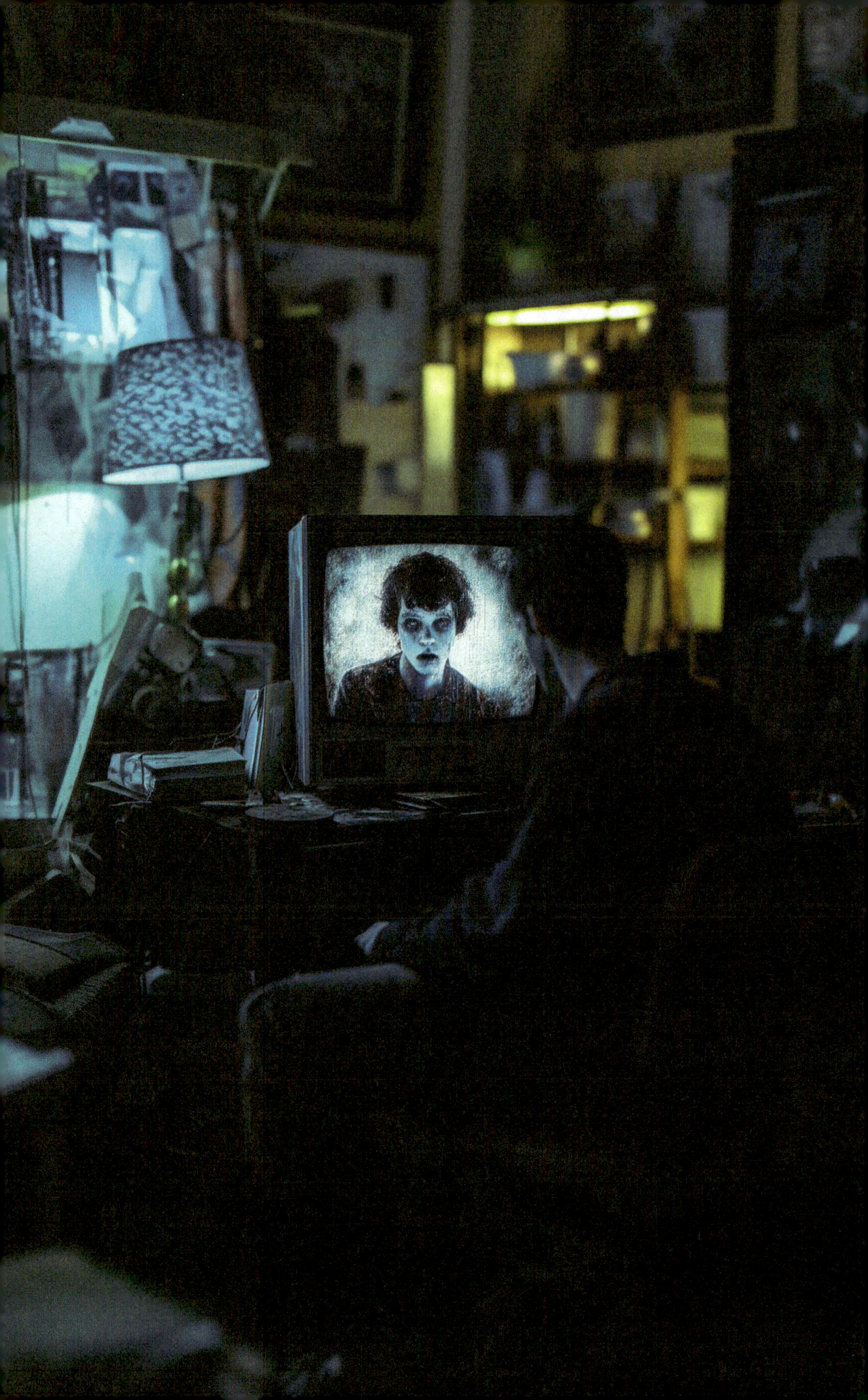

"Noah?" Liam whispered, leaning closer.

The screen crackled, and there he was. Noah's face twisted in the static, his head now a television, eyes black and hollow.

"Liam," Noah rasped. "It listens. The static... it listens to us."

Liam froze. "What do you mean?"

Noah's face flickered. "It watches. It studies us. Every time you watch, it watches back. Don't trust it. Don't let it in."

Liam's hand hovered over the cord, trembling.

Noah's voice cracked, barely a whisper. "Unplug it. Now. Before it's too late."

Then, softer still: "It's already listening."

The screen went black.